MONKEY-TOWN

MONKEY-TOWN

CARRIE CHANG

Library of Congress Control Number: 2015914966
ISBN: Hardcover   978-1-5035-8683-3
                   Softcover   978-1-5035-8682-6
                   eBook   978-1-50358-681-9

Print information available on the last page.

Rev. date: 09/11/2015

To order additional copies of this book, contact:
Xlibris
1-888-795-4274
www.Xlibris.com
Orders@Xlibris.com
719739

CONTENTS

This book is dedicated to the memory of my grandfather,
Chang-Chih-Ho, who taught me the meaning of love and life.

PART I

THE SHAMAN'S PROPHECY

From its imperial, good-for-nothing bamboo seats to its wizardly people with their crabby, upturned noses to its parakeet rice, which makes you go half stir-crazy, Monkey-town, with its unpredictable yawps and mawkish yips, allows the native brown eye to roll away on a Thursday evening when the ginseng-colored people are ambling down on Geary Street under the fractured moon as the sounds of spice buckets and dim sum huts makes the yellow heart go bitter weak.

In a spigot of purple mist, the monkey men play their fabulous instruments dreamily with a *tsing* and a zap, while the sere buff clouds overhead impart a rose-colored rain. After all, all in the city is *zazen* and afterlife, with a smidgen of contempt for famed onlookers. There was the final deluge of cosmic fingerprints on the overgrown cactus in the backyard of Yeo's and virtuoso singing coming from the frappé windows of the castlelike apartments, which were covered with the thick of frothy pastel paint. "Come, Master Shaman, come!" calls out the deciduous, one-eared monk from the nearby temple, banging his supercilious brassy gong. The dolorous slight jaybirds quietly slurp their pikay seeds in sweet slumber.

In the lamplight, the broken rainbow of sampan lusts tenets over the whole city, while its denizens sleep quietly, dreaming of medicine of the heart, turning fitfully in a brocade of weighty matters, their dark nostrils piqued by the aroma of incense and reverie. There was, of course, the variety of what the famous sandman would bring in tomorrow, of whose dream would be fulfilled with a pash of light, of what rays would shine on the flashy aureole of the anointed children of the entire fabled town. The harpy dragon flies through the oval window, with thick unctuous breath on its lavender scales, warning the people of their outright heresy.

At the super-karmic zoo, weepy arms and weepy legs pour out of the creepy seesaw aquarium of time and move like kettle-fish, glistening genie gold. Wab ghosts rattle in the basement, and imaginary hot congee thickens with despotic suspense in an obstreperous dream world, laughing in the oceanic fog. What matters is the disingenuous smile of bewitched sailors, the rigmarole of sheepish denizens moving about in iridescent circles of yore.

Here, the impossible smell of kung pao chicken makes one lurch forward for one's chopsticks, knitting stories in a shock-hot fantasy, as six-prong dice and ruby-colored fingers make one merry in the next room at Yeo's, where the action is always heavy. Lured by the lozenges of light in the waxy lilac wallpaper and the smell of pure cognac, I order my variety of dishes, a moiety of blush on my round fabled cheeks.

It's the pure sanctity of the place that keeps me coming back for more, for the lovely saffron rice and the jade-scented bok choy as we hear the *pipa* playing melodiously for the countless time inside. With its telltale lotus signs and its magical scent of ambergris, I drink up at Yeo's diner and finger my chubby bubble teas, jeering the shimmering jellies of tapioca to worm up on my pink tongue. It's a holiday binge, some cleft of the mind for the happy gourmand, some tilt to the kung fu heart to be sure.

Why the women are so sad, living spare-dream lives that are balefully parceled out for the angel cherubs of subway fantasies, chewing on shredded celery and chicory sticks in their extra time, and complaining about the devil-may-care weather. Why the men choose to wear bowler derbies made of cheap felt and smoke their to-do cigars with a bit of panache on the spur? Why the derby seaside weather leaves you feeling so downright depressed and full of conniptions and verve? Such deep gunshot feelings so as not to be put down in a consummate frenzy.

The orchid-lipstick women pack their succor wares on Boulder Street with depressed hues of mercy leaving a blotter of disgrace in midair; they're always channeling waves like that, beta-breakers of surprise from onlookers with their succulent waves, their curvy smiles in the soft light. One small break, and it could be their choleric eyes opening with poise, charming the whole world with a mystical wonder. Their caustic glow is like little Buddha's touch, that glitter beyond reproach, some *ra-ta-ta-ta* of the skeleton finger beyond the open-and-shut closet.

The sass of the dragon ladies in the spiritual cloud of forgotten stitch will enchant tourists, as do the jade pieces of the faux Ming vases beguile double-spawn; with reddish hyacinth hues, those contours of mishmash art of past dynasties find themselves on display near the toy store on Clay Street as signs of another world, the forgotten beat era.

With chewed-up betel nut in the silvery cracks of the sidewalks and some sassafras on the tongues of the shih tzus, the infernal beat goes on as the leathery peanuts glimmer in the sunshine with circuslike vanity. Why try to understand it, the spidery splotch of calligraphy on the metro station, which passes as outright Chinese? Why try to break those delimiters of geography, stretching past susurrus clouds of nether-zero? Bother to see those in situ spacey elements of wind and moon, which cross over into the city and ruin the whole thing?

I'd like to think of Mr. Lim's toy store as the hazy place where the toy clock spins out its delicious numbers of bingo and the smiles of miniature nutcrackers doing their usual spondee digits with automatic luster, the famous laundry store where the frosted elements turn and toss in the driers until they become cherry-blind, the caterpillar dust on the bright pillowcases turning into lighter bronze. All these are symptomatic of the kind of distractions you'll find in the city—the beat-up velveteen dresses and upturned noses, the rice cookers with offbeat sausages in them, and the blessings of pious plenty.

It's well known that the women of Monkey-town wear shoulder-strap *chongsams*, purple silk in the moonlight with bangs and play their one-up cards in smoky, unkempt rooms, their eye shadow crooked and their lips warbling with accents like fish. Their dull eyes ooze with compunction about the final blessed hour, and as the chefs do their hocus-pocus with steaming squid fried rice, they use their push-up bras like accordions, with winning guts, scouting out the itsy-bitsy mosquitoes in their mai tai drinks. Their spider drinks in tow. How seething are their looks, and with what juicy venom do they paint their toes—a wowsy ochre or a dainty red—as if done in bread box with holes, as in a cartoonish dab.

"How awesome are the Buddha's callings!" cries out the one-eared monk, banging his brass gong as if to wake the neighborhood up. His words rake the purling wind and send scattered leaves purling over the trick bricks as if to cover them with meretricious gold, the faux cobblestones.

Like spiritual animé, the fish-kettle pouf blows its smoke out the chestnut door, and the green-mint umbrellas in the water spin vertiginously. The snaky light of spoons meanders along the dragonlike bodies of the women who play their cards with raucous laughter. Outside, on Waverly Street, the yew trees glisten with bronze sap. The supernatural fabric of fowl and finch felt upon the earth, with gimlet mosquitoes calling into question the foul weather. The weird mimelike motions of the women are like ticktock wind-up toys, the legerdemain of the Far East, not to mention this idle talk of incestuous strangers.

"I guess you call it into question, the magic of Monkey-town," says the shaman, pouting, his arms akimbo, his sorry shadow incomplete, standing in the doorway at Waverly Street, gnats all about his clean, moth-eaten face. "The magic of the monkey men is without question!"

The stud marks of the callow witches and warlords of the place make me wince entirely over their precious congee, over their haloed remarks, reminding one of lost footnotes from the desiccated crypt. Like flirtatious hyenas, they suspend life with a fried bit of affectations and hubris. It hurts them because they're crying so damned hard. Their scintillating hair stands up on end like the flyaway punctuation of the beats.

With both chopsticks knitting legends of blasé color, it's then that they feast on ideas of the past and the future, dripping beads of red soy on their toes. How is it, they say, that the moon shines, as an operative dime in the slot machine, push-coin heavy? In their plumlike antiquity, they walk about on these fairy-tale clogs and muck-it up, their slim damper eyes turning to high heaven.

I could reveal to you my inner feelings of Monkey-town in a solitary thud, only to converse with you for a few moments about the simple rose-colored tablecloths on fire, about the stringy, disenchanted women, about Mr. Fong's wild rants into town and their black arts phenomenon. All was a wild rainbow fix, this rambunctious ride into nowhere. Their cheap, dapper hats they tipped to the Buddha but were surprised when they flew off in the sequined wind, the grasshopper's continuous *tsin g*in the electric filthy air.

***

Of course, I remember Mr. Fong and his philosophical rants, his ragtime charm and his chocolate-colored fedora, his ginseng nose turning wild colors in the wind, his heavy tread and the chortling of his Cantonese, the way the shopkeepers would stare at him as if he were a heavy artifact in bas-relief shining in the faded, dried-out sun, and his eager skin like a scaly antidote to quarrelsome remarks about old men's beauty. *Lang zhai! That hot young man I used to be!*

Them ginger-colored folk, that's what they were, the tiny people of Monkey-town brushing their teeth fastidiously on a holiday or staring at you squeamishly from their four-eye lenses in the orange buff. What made them so special was their utter hospitality, their utter saintliness, and their foolish egalitarian pride. I'd like to add that the people of Monkey-town were enraged by their state of native allowance and spoke lightly of their plight, scooping many dollops of rice into their plates with upturned noses.

"Well, it'll be that, the *moo goo gai pan* tonight or the winter melon soup!" Mrs. Wong would say tenderly to herself, buttering up her dayroom curls and moving her dishpan outside her window at precisely four in the afternoon. Such utter desperation in her spindle eyes as a tiny goldfish was curled up in her spoon!

You could say it was the vanity in their hearts that made them think twice before leaving its red arches, marching outside of its perimeters into San Francisco. Like a *paradiso* with gilded doors, Monkey-town promised to be a conundrum of starched metaphors, an angelic house of children fated to be christened with sundry haw flakes and coconut stems in their mouths and lizard bandages on their feet. In good and inclement weather, they would stroll down Jackson Street past the tickertape of

Monkey-town, culpable for being villains of sorrow, so strange their elongated stares and their lofty ways that they transcended the classes they came from and dreamt of old Mother China in rich, vibrant hues. They rode the oriental carpet in midair as if they were flying to Mars and were indeed behest of some myriad dragons that spoke to them darkly: *speak deep and heed the shaman's words! Speak deeply, and be that outrageous!*

Like the anxious parakeet who fluttered inside Yeo's and had countless, eternal daydreams and tittered on a high-sass note, the smug-faced patrons of Monkey-town who sported checked derbies and glossy raincoats and polka-dot trousers mimicked the *caw* of the bird and did double takes of everything they did, noting the dreamlike quality of Monkey-town's vibrato-like quietude: the flirty aftertaste of the 7 Up, the pow-pow of the rice, and the queasy colors of the moon-hued *mah-poh tofu*. Good plain luck came in rivulets of power, in pockets of propinquity. It didn't matter whether you were just playing around or *serious* about your work. Everyone who passed under the branches of the yew tree on Kearny Street was *zapped* on the head with magical powers of the heavens and given a new name, like Rosie, Carmichael, or Madonna. Life floated in and out the windows like the ether dragon, who snorted so easily as to find new super luck in the penumbra of the sordid heavens, and the magic dice was rolled by the newcomers with their sticky caramel fingers.

****

Monkey-town as a fabulist zero town, as a spigot of rose and thorns, an awkward destiny seen at the end of a drainpipe of sorts. The colors of an octopus whorl unsettle me, and I'm at my fantasy again, driving down Highway 101 toward Monkey-town, about to cross the bridge to enter the forbidden portal of sweet gilded arches through tea-smoke and oranges to become the seeker of pure time and history.

As deep testament to my madness and my stealthier agues, I was searching my beat, getting my acupuncture done on Jackson Street weekly, taking my set of paradise pills, of dragon root, ginger stew, and daisy stem variety of malarkey for instant pep in that limestone fairy jungle. Having my share of catfish stew and dancing with the viridian crickets under the signs at Polk Street where the electric gizmo cages rattle with some bit of fortitude.

"You know you've reached the other Oz, the end of the rainbow," confessed the shaman, walking on tea-colored eggshells with his bare feet one day on Polk Street and noticing my staid melancholia. He pointed to the rest of the gossamer street signs in Monkey-town and suggested that I should trace them with my naked hand.

"There's magic in this phoenix villa, a cloud wrack of beauty in every nook and cranny. Just look, this cricket is singing an aria that could turn your heart inside out!"

I felt suddenly sullen, as if the sci-fi light of the entire city had flooded my ken and made the town into a roaming circus of sorts, ersatz color, so rife with mayhem, a ballyhoo of the nouveau century. It was the foolish wonderment of the wuthering people, with their little Buddha heads, as if brought down from on cloud high that made them wonder of their frankness, of their keen noblesse oblige.

For Monkey-town was a plentiful fountain of dreams and true believers, a world of bubblegum blowers who saw painful hues in their powerful words and walked a tightrope between light and heavy, big and small, and tall and short. They spoke with a chop-chop fancy and deliberated with long breaths before coming down on the unsolvable answer floating in sync. There was some bedevilment in their pose, which rained down rosy and spare, like the tattered legs of hairy spiders and the argot of genies. It didn't matter who said what, like a play in which there was a thimble of silver in every tortured line. It all shimmered like a fairy-tale loom to be sure.

With pinched foreheads and pockets full of moonbeams, the beautiful people of Monkey-town came originally in ships from La Chine and spoke Toisanese in the dusk with a raspy stare, so starkly beautiful that there were hot sparks in the air. A chancy sputter in the wok, a guttural play on words. An iota of a missive written with soy sauce on a crumpled napkin. Like a kitschy kiss from the monkey men's lips, everything about the place was lit up, like the two-way mirror of a gimcrack fantasy, so lividly purple that it made you dance on salty toothpicks.

These were my cultural hors d'oeuvres, my sangfroid with the fish belly straight up. The gigging clown in Mr. Lim's toy shop showed his greaselike fangs and rolled his belly, exciting the children to no end; the stuffed monkeys and tin drums too chimed in the candied window like some treat to the eye, pickled humor for the tumescent soul. And with a smile, I returned to my place at Yeo's, fingering the corpse of a bok choy, like a lustrous jade in tow, and strutting through the oval window, lusting after more rice like a ferule bandit. It was the blinking disco music with its neurotic beats that did me in, made me giddy in the head like Diana Ross; and as I twirled my chopsticks in the air with a batonlike effect, I could see the nirvana of Monkey-town through my glass tumbler, apple green and wondrous, refracting like a world of gluey monikers and mischief.

****

What distinguishes Monkey-town from other cities is its cache of rubies, its tapering sixteen-inch zebra nails, and its oilskin snake drums banging into the starry heavens. The frowning debutantes with the Mona Lisa telltale smile on Mercy Street rub their jades and look into the fairy-tale cosmos for rain. A cracked Ming vase puffed up in the opiate light, my kink curls in druthers, ruddy kneesocks on fire. I had come to understand it—their love for creamy phoenix eyes, for mystery, for the carnal beauty of the world. What made it deeper was this fictive hole in the universe they were stuck in, this C-town, this final blow into smoke rings, some lost rhythm of a song they could hear playing through the sewer streets of yore.

"I've heard stranger music, gypsy music played by darker peoples than ours but none as sorrowful!" says the pock-faced woman who was selling her wares, a half-gutted catfish with a stony eye and a bouquet of vegetables by the pound. Her eyes, half-almond, a monolid of bestial proportions, fluttered like a moth off of clean paper. Her pale blue shirt, a scrim of button-up pride, stuck to her curved back, bending over like a huge mountain.

"A sop of plenty! A sop for my people!" exclaims the monk, banging his gong to no end.

"I can see you're an outsider, that you speak Chinese like a baby," says Mr. Fong one afternoon, guffawing with his arms sideways in the hyacinth-colored wind. "What brings you to Monkey-town?"

"Just to pass the time and to taste the red bean desserts, to catch a glimpse of all that craziness!" I say back, noticing the rowdiness of the traffic, how the bird-blue Buick almost bumps into another car and crashes. "To go with the Tao!"

At Yeo's, the white congee is glistening gold, and the oolong tea-colored fantasies stain the pages of *Watermark* and *Dream of the Red Mansions*. The parakeet is decidedly nonplussed and howl sits operettas at a high bawdy pitch, like some opera star, and the customers carouse and poke at their sticky rice balls with their long chopsticks like crazy surgeons on the fix, looking for water chestnuts and frog intestines to gulped down with a slurpy relish. They are *crazed*, full of mean venom, a brittle bevy of nonstop kvetchers with wagging tongues that crush their lychee and longan with a shiver. The sully eyed waitress with the shrill voice screams *yut-ge, yut-ge*, and the bamboo fritters arrive, one by one, in their loveliness, steaming to the top. All in all, a consummate to-do for the big nosh.

Dabbling in the square of his *gufu*, the young scholar Ming blows some mosquito glitter off his left nostril and, with wet eyes, dreams of far-off archipelagoes, imagines some thimble-like dolls made of clay, some warriors or sampan witches of Cathay that titillate with bit eyes and smiles made of spooled thread. With a nostalgic push, he moves his pen in the *gufu* and writes with an octopus whorl of ink, of old-time magic, of sweet red bean in his mouth, and of better times. The rice paper shimmers like some ghetto blanket, and all his *gufus* look like windows of candid memory.

Monkey-town must surely seem dream-heavy, like one huge existential slurp from a silver straw, a stem from a cosmic fried coconut. Frenzied, harried, quixotic, harpish, and with angelic slumber on their doughty faces, Chinese people of this town rockabilly to sleep with thoughts of ecstasy on their faces, each jade breath exploding into other worlds.

"It must be strange to strut in here unnoticed and take in all that local color and posh," says the monk to me, grinning. "You must be misunderstood!"

"You must be dying for another plate of rice," says Ming in a bored voice, rolling his pinprick eyes, which project into the seer of the future. "Order black bean next time!"

"What is the meaning of Monkey-town, and why are its people so outrageous?" I ask him, but he only shrugs his no-nonsense shoulders as if to say, "Get outta here!" and simpers, "It's not for the weak—only the monomaniacs can understand the place. Read the graffiti on the walls, get a hint, *shrug*."

I chortle sarcastically as if I retained the gist of his meaning but inside am still confused—with its fantine windows and its syllabic beat, Monkey-town is like the Garden of Eden unplugged, some overaged apple core in the night, but the ghostlike people meander about with such flirty oversized hats as to be hilarious and bawdy, full of streetlight venom, all stop 'n' go. I want to put the amber spotlight on them to make them speak of their history, but in their mouths is all *yut, ye, sam,* and burnished lingo of the stars. The candor of the lone dragon making its way out of the teacup, whose fragile lines crack like a prehistoric Easter egg.

Giving birth to confetti-like struggles in the dark, the people of Monkey-town are perturbed by the wavy sunsets of the world, the way in which the hair of the women shine at night like wixwax or soy sauce in a jar; what makes the shih tzus growl with maybilly dishonor. The yew trees shiver like women without minks. The laughing children with commas in their eyes stomp their feet at Washington Park, where the seesaw is driven by the up and down of those squalid bodies.

Tossing straight-laced tassel caps with the gold fringe into the sea, the whorl-faced Monkey-men, who long to be kissed, show me their grim smiles of ancient sorrow, and the dragon moves like a housefly into the musty tenements, gathering mud. Electric skeletons do their dance with a flourish as if every day were Halloween, and the ointment-covered preachers scream their sermons from Clay Street, jibing their parishioners.

With mummy masks fastened on tight, they drink their cricket juice, oozing from the center of their foppish teeth, and speak the *lingua franca* of the Chinese specimen in modern times. These pelican-masked women who swoon in the mirror and stab their white *baos* with panache and bandy about on leather feet who swear they'll know no other in the trefoil of the yew trees, these slim cats of destruction who walk blithely and speak of beautiful disorder as a fact of the cosmos.

***

Continuous muttering in the gag box of time, the gangly limbs of a velveteen monkey in tow dancing with a gnarled rope, the seaside honor of the Cantonese matrons with shiny curls, thumb-covered photographs ripped in two. The birdseed glittering under the orblike sun. The ivory beach seething beneath your elephant feet at last. The chestnut-colored faces overlooking you in the far distance.

Surely as the moon is a punch-out tool, and the *Om*-chasers will divulge their well-kept secrets tonight; I'll take my fancy flight to Chinatown for a meandering chase of local color and a wonton killer, some seeds of high propinquity which have put me to slumber. I'll drink that toxic gin and twiddle my thumbs, curl up like moss, and seethe for a good few moments, dulling the stupor senses. How the fish-kettles of the old women of Shanghai knock together like wrinkled knees and sing the fantastic fables of yore, of the secret moody script of the Far East and the myriad creatures of the penetrating sea.

Of fire cracker frenzy and the fiery digitalis of the moon, of the specious calling of the wizards in perfect tinfoil hats, of the sputtering spasmodic "O" of the sea dragon and sleepy wicker fish. The mosslike hair of the phoenix dolls, their eyes, ready for the crypt at last. The silkworm hanging just off the top of the seaside roof, the warped solo of birds chirping their oracle in phantom play, the off-the-cuff remarks of the innocent bystanders.

How the old women in their kneesocks weed their bronze dough, moving with humility, a hint of playfulness in their Manchurian threads, with a plaid stitch of irony. How the men amble about with their thrice-colored birdcages, telling time with glossy feet and pretend they are shadows of dishonor, sages from another world, another time. Another try at so-called reincarnation.

I say I am halfway there, to point B, the destination of madness and honor, to understanding Chinatown's prowess, to being a true gamin of worth. The meaning of the city escapes me still with its half-open windows, its heyday weather, and its damnable truths. The perturbed women look at their horoscope palms in horror and count the minutes till they've arrived at their destination on their lifeline. I mean, really, where is the trompe l'oeil I'm missing? Where do sun and moon collide? How do the people come and go without missing a beat? Where does the rose-colored fog land on the sequined brows of the people, causing them to shudder *in extremis?*

*****

The pitter-patter of the bitter rain, the umbrageous shadows on the drainpipe, the color of sweat on the humidifier. At Yeo's, the plates spin like flying saucers, while the waiters sing *yut-ge, yut-ge,* the chomp noodles shimmering like some hair of throaty, nuff back angels. With an inch of anticipation, I dig in, eat up the pastries that make my knees fat with a sesame-seeded anger, and gaze out at the beacon of the moon. Too much to say it, what makes the entire world go round with a spoon— that gaseous attack of laughter after the winter melon soup spooked me, making me glow swimmingly with pride.

"I tell you, Master Wu, there are places that serve food as delicious as C-town but not many!" exclaims the shaman with some soggy crab legs in his mouth, some manna as foul beast. His hair dampened as the copper fish in the river.

As he speaks to me this way, his fake ivory teeth glisten like some keen parable of joy, and lilacs bloom effusively in a stiff-necked vase. There is much quackery in this place, where people come to get their deep fix, their sacrilegious play. Incense-heavy, Monkey-town is rife with supernatural drivel, with belladonnas in their predicate guise.

"I say to you, that the people here are as thin as thimbles and as brilliant as aspidistras!" says the shaman again, chomping into his succulent chow mein and bean sprouts, the Bodhisattvas in the pillows lolling their shrill pink tongues out at him with hellish flair.

His very skinny words are gold ingots bright as flames, boulders running over my florid body. I am loathed to explain why I look at him suspiciously, as I do everything in Monkey-town, which is like a beautiful, cheap tattoo of red and viridian colors. Some smatter of carnal paints that point to high heaven. A to-do chop shop of snakelike venom, a bevy of cricket soldiers marching in the dark.

"Not to press you, but you have an astounding heart!" he says, snorting, eating the rest of his *boy choy* with a slow burp. As he eats, the swarthy hair of his piques on end, like some electric zither in the wind, and his chops flutter. Like a sampan man with a twitch of pouty exclamation about him. He is a holy man.

Bristling with energy, I've found something in that cracked jade of a city, some "save the world", la-di-da quotient to pepper my dreams, some slight formula for brief, undulating words to queue the sandman with. When I go sleep later that night, I'm overcome with smiling grief, ecstatic tears, dreaming of being zapped by white light, by the curvaceous waves of the purling ocean where the astounded denizens of Monkey-town are dancing with upturned shoes and the sleepy lotus factory of dice and mangosteen. I'm smiling like a child, wondering where the alpha and the omega are.

***

Some baubles, roughed up on the edges; the chimera, of lost causes; the noodle factory on Jackson and Market, where the yuppies on the edge of roiling angst go. The neon *cha-sui* or steamed pork that makes you go *agog* with a thousand tears; those frank promises of the young imprimatur of love in spring, moving about in a cloud of gusto, the contralto of squalls in the den wharf. All these come to mind as we wander to the careless perimeter of Monkey-town on a Sunday, the clouds raining heavy news on the shimmer of plane trees, trees which shake and tremble like transparent tumblers.

I do not know where I'd go without that turnpike on 80 past the Bay Bridge, taking notice of the red apple lantern sign on the right, into *oriental ville.* Alias Monkey-town. A moniker of true grace to be sure. I push the pedal hard and get to Market Street and make a left on Clay up the hill until I see all the tacky neon signs, smell all the barbecue fried rice joints that leave me starved plenty, and then park right under Washington Park, past the butterfly mantras woven into the air and the devil-may-care graffiti that glisten with a salty kopek. And then I walk straight into the staid portal of another world where the tangerine sparks of the damp vehicles send spurts of cosmic wonder into the air. I'm headed for Yeo's, the land of barnaby eats and sly wonder funk.

"To think it, that you come here for the freebies, the nightlife, and the doo-wop glam," says Mrs. Wong, a comical ingénue, brightening in the twizzled spotlight, doing her milky nails with a seedy varnish. "To think that you bring everything to this place!"

There is for sure some comely turtle-colored vanity in her persimmon curls as embellished cue in her voice, which reminds me fondly of my grandma, how she shoulders the world like an exotic poncho, and junks her scanty fish bones in the miniature milk box, hiccupping wildly. Her patient nostrils flare out like a fattish poodle in vivid heat, and her ginger lips speak of the first millennia, disappearing in a weeping flash of white light.

As I pepper my oxtail's soup with a bit of angst, I think back to the many vignettes of my so-called life and, with a practiced grin, begin to soul-search after all these years for an identity to call my own. I pick at the vainglorious rice on my plate, a wandering genie in the desperate search of a talisman, some purposeful mark of destiny on this fabled earth.

"Tell me more," says the shaman, with open eyes, rubbing the jade on his chest with embalmed apoplexy. "What are you seeking, and why do you come here?"

The wicked bamboo chairs creak back and forth, and the scrubby-faced people look at me with daft curiosity. The mealy mouthed waiter, with his mop of hair, stops serving his wild stubby orange lobsters and looks my direction with outcast eyes to see what words I'll say. The whole restaurant seems suddenly quiet then, as I'm caught in the spotlight.

I glare insensibly at the patrons and then mutter a few nonsensical statements about my propinquity until they look away with the shaman appearing nonplussed. It seems a shame to say so much about a taboo topic that rattles the brain to the very hilt.

I took my cue from mongers, from flashy-assed monkeys, from two-bit hairdressers, from any of those circus creatures of the moon. Mine was the world of spoony creatures of ersatz reality, of those doo-wop spiders that sing piperly in the dark. It is a fine thing to speak of other cosmos, of other subconscious layers of dust rising in the opium den to smoke the bamboo pipe smugly and to laugh at the bugaboos that are desperate for your attention.

With flayed, juicy fingers pointing to the viridian stars, I took flight to Monkey-town for many reasons: to taste the oily, chopped greens of fresh vegetables that might cure me of lost love, some mystical foundling twist of the genie I had found in the soy sauce can that twinkled my wispy eye, the funny crack of the fortune cookie that made me laugh, and the gutted fish that spewed some pithy verbs of sampan light. It was that hidden value in the trashy hexagonal shadows that made me oddly mum and think of the shaman's outrage and say no more.

****

At Felicia's Best, a woman's hat shop on Waverly Street, the pale mannequins glow faintly with their sanitized eyes and their wormy acute smiles, wearing the several patched-up dresses imported from the Mainland. Crisp, amorous browns, and fresh caterpillar greens, oceanic blues, and candy cane stripes that make your eyes pop out dizygotically with much ado. Serious-about-me colors that you see in those turn-of-the-century dramas in which the woman speaks with an afternoon lisp and pats her hair every second with an eccentric gusto. I want to shake her and make her realize that her mother is spying on her and will probably rip up her best letters, ruin everything for her and her lover in the next episode. Those *cha-cha-cha* dramas are full of psychopomp and much to do played all over outer Chinatown with a gimlet rose effect. The bargain basement tapes are worth perhaps every cent.

At Felicia's, the shimmer of fake roses melt in the ghoulish light, picked at by loud, aping fingers, and the stiff black leather belts are so peevishly small that they are for life-size Barbie dolls that say mew. The pinched brown shoes are the stuff of Suzy Wong fantasies, the hologram pillbox hats also, some Eastern-Western cool effect that is antiquated as chilled romantic dust, some turn-of-the-screw haze that makes you scream when you wear them, scratchy in the hose and cloudy blue in the nose. The chintzy velveteen buttons are duly priceless, unctuous knickknacks you can put in your purse, and the lovely stickpins—these too have a fickle, floral appeal, giving you that priceless, starved-loving glimmer of sorts. Covered with radar webs, you feel that spider effect in your best Pinochet, smelling like damp aspirin and mothballs, super-clammy to the very end.

"We have no *chongsams* here," says Mrs. Yu, the proprietor of Felicia's. "For that kind of thing, look down the street at Sammy's!" she says saucily, with a sudden clap.

Sammy's is all about that flossy stuff, that birdcage trope that people love on winter days after drinking their tiny cup of oolong tea broth. Some fake *bindi* nails or peacock eyelashes or silk ottomans imported directly from Turkey or Shanghai. Anything with a jester's touch or a virulently purple powder they take in. With a dreamy look in my eye, I walk down Waverly Place and enter Sammy's, only to see Mr. Yee, saying *tsk, tsk* at the sound of my lousy Western accent.

"Why can't you speak good Cantonese?" he asks, growling, his slanted eyes bulging like a blowfish, teasing me.

"I'm a bamboo child," I say, pouting. "Dwei um ju!"

"What are you doing in town—just hanging around?"

"I'm here to see the shaman."

"Don't listen to the shaman—he's a good for nothing, son of a bitch!"

"Why are you saying that? He seems like a good guy."

"Lousy son of a bitch! Doesn't pay up during mah-jongg!"

I cringe and walk away, glimpsing at the setup of all the gigantic pearls on display on the shelf, huge Mongolian pearls which glimmer with a deep bony inveterate hue, some inlaid flamboyant bamboo headdress. These flighty peacock dresses, the flashy feathers that fly to the moon, the cheap-looking jade pedants that change eerie colors in the penultimate bourse, and of course, the silky *chongsams* look like roaming catfishes about to swim away in the rushing water. So flimsy and covered with embroidery that one imagines oneself being squeezed to death in one consummate wear—so tight as to be choked like a paper accordion in full uptux.

"I see you outsiders coming back into Monkey-town looking for one thing—and that's trouble!" says Mr. Yee, brushing his silk sleeve with naked fingers. "It's this thing to be respectful. And humble. Not just chasing the Tao with a broom."

"I'm just here for the gossip and the bubble teas, that's all," I lie, laughing, adding that I seem to come for my acupuncturist. "It's nothing that deep, you see."

As the loud bugle horn bursts outside, the shih tzu gives out a low moan, and Mr. Yee suddenly raids me an odd, vulgar stare and asks how my mother is and lets me out the front door, saying, in that tight-lipped, no-nonsense voice all the proprietors have, "Have a nice day. Come back again." As the day falls, I walk out the door in a violent frenzy, the rainbow confetti rain falling all over my surprised face.

****

Sleepy peaches with their brilliantine nectar haunt me deeply, as do my lesser depressive agues, as I return to that crystal bailiwick to seethe my woes. It's been days since I've talked to the shaman, and my entire head reverberates with a painful *om*, a sort of damp holy echo of the frantic gods. I stare at the streetlights with a wide-eyed fantasy, meditating on *yellow* for caution, and step into busy traffic with a sure vain foot. The blue pebbles splash in my face, showing my cartoonish bewilderment at the common world.

"Why in such a hurry?" asks Mr. Fong, his cracked yellow teeth showing in a pensive smile as he walks quickly by in-checked plaid pants and leathery shoes which are the color of pandy. His bushy, string-up eyebrows look like hairy Scotch tape; his pale lips quiver like goose lips of ether.

"I'm looking for the shaman. Have you seen him?"

"He's sleeping. He's at the in the Hotel L'Orange."

"Where can I find him?"

"It's on Geary and Fifth. You can't miss it!"

I thank Mr. Fong profusely and hurry along on my way, pass the old beat-up cars and the itinerant sway of blooming yew trees past the fire hydrants and the old mystic temple where the svelte-eyed monks are congregating together, smoking hist. "If you see the shaman, tell him that we are witnessing great miracles!" says the one-eared monk sheepishly, banging on his brass gong and gnawing on some disfigured wheat. *Monkey-town is waking up!*

I tend to agree and think to myself that true mysticism is in the works, a leather snake winding across the wide river of time, some antiquarian rattle that will shake minds and hearts and make the people of Monkey-town live through whorls of smoke, see fish in their gin-tonic, and make lotuses bloom fretfully again into shavers. Like the coming of a new century in the chatter throes of a late, great awakening.

"Where is the shaman?" asks the monk again, gagging out loud. "His speeches are priceless to us! Fetch him, young girl!"

I nod and press on to Geary Street where I see a battered old hotel with dreadful lurid graffiti on the wall, the kind of dupy motor inn which sits empty for the most part, except for passing ghosts, I suspect. The outside is a hideous orange taupe, and the front lobby has a sad-looking yucca tree matching the extraordinarily *rude* décor precisely, some knobby nude paintings from Bosch, and an old woman yawning at the front desk.

"Did you see the shaman come in here?" I ask tentatively, quaking with some nervous laughter.

"On the seventh floor!" she replies drily, giving me the droll eye and looking wicked. "Room B."

I then climb the old wooden stairs, which creak incessantly, up and down, and circle around, thinking of all the holy, inane things the shaman has said to me, of his profound jokes, his riddles, and his cryptic departures. Lofty, lofty indeed!

As I reach the seventh floor, I walk to room B, which is half open. There's a coddle of carnal smoke pouring out to the sound of what perceived to be the breathing of a man and woman in heavy copulation, making loud whoopee.

As I quickly rap on the door, I notice it's the shaman with Mrs. Yu, from Felicia's hat store, who is half naked, with a shocked look on her face. The two tumble from the bed and quickly get dressed and scream for quick cover.

"Don't tell my husband!" screams Mrs. Yu, who is sore and mad as bricks.

"Look here, what's this about?" says the shaman, recovered and dressed with his angelic taut face covered with sweat, his body showing his snake tattoo on his arm. "Why are you here at this time of the day?"

He then yawns, a bit miffed, and opens his pocket and picks out a coin which says *lucky me*, handing it obliquely to me. He says, "Go tell those monks the feng shui has changed directions. The Tao is bending with the light. Deposit this coin in the spittoon *at Master Charlie's*, and you'll be duly blessed."

As he yawns, again, blushing, he blesses me and tells me to go and shuts the door, snoring; and I run down the stairs with the small magic coin in my pocket and a studious look in my two big frozen eyes. The woman at the counter gives me an honorific stare, only to dismiss me as a hoaxer.

"What would give a million stars to know the secrets of the greats?" she says, sarcastically as I walk quickly out the door.

As the driver wind blows my long hair into a million strands of blackness, I press the coin into my frosty palm and whistle, dreaming of those lotuses and bracken, of the many fragile teacups of the dowagers of yore and the pestle and mortar of those wild apothecaries who knew how to cure people of the Chinatown blues. Such melancholia in my eyes as I walk down Market Street that I begin to weep profuse, corrupt tears, to sing the songs of the *erhu*, and to head down to Yeo's for some afternoon dim sum, *sup-sup*. The thought of some *dan tat*, some shrimp toast could cure a person of the roller-coaster bum-out and bring some of that spring fever back again.

***

The next morning, I awaken in dreams of kudzu and junkie roses and press the lucky coin to my outer palm, laughing outright. What could the so-called shaman's prophecy mean? *Never mind*, I say, putting it in my coat pocket, rushing to the call of morning breakfast. My mother, who is age sixty-four, telephones me up and asks why I'm always gone, and I tell her I'm constantly swinging off to the city of Chinatown to see the acupuncturist, that I've been knocking about the dusty enclave discovering new lights to the entire siven world. Some damned monkey mix of spiritual meandering that keeps me on my clever toes upright at first.

"Why Chinatown?" she asks nervously, tittering on the phone like haystack. "Why not a local doctor? You spend too much time there and are just asking for trouble. It's a no-good place!"

"I like it—the funky beat of it all, the dim sum, the neon lights, the disco parlors."

"It's a no-man's town—a no-good place for people like you! Just asking for trouble!" she snaps at me, sounding verily impatient, and asks me if I talked to Mr. Yee.

"Yes, I went to Sammy's, and he said hello," I confess, sounding bored. These Chinatown folks all know my mom and the way she goes about buying up the place, with her bok choy fetish.

"Well, that's fine, but just don't go so often and get more sleep and stop smoking so much!"

"That's right, Ma."

With religious, down-home teeth and sampan eyes, my mother was a breathing Cantonese woman with flighty bones, the kind of sprite that could make a man laugh with her trilling p's and q's, floating in and out of doors like a nervy witch on a broom. Telling old age has made her twice as nervy, with a twitch of the mean thumb, eyes as mild as winding rivers and hair as thick as an old forest. With a face like a round peony, she is charming in her broken English, her feigned alacrity, her floury jetsam smile. Like a wily snake of hours, she wears the fake jade my grandmother gave her around her neck and lives in Foster City, where she whiles the hours like a matron of plenty.

"Didn't I tell you, Jenna, that Chinatown is full of ghosts that will rattle you, make you *feng* or crazy?"

I promise her, lying a bit, that I won't go to San Francisco so much and hang up the phone, feeling more depressed. It's those conversations with the personals that will get you down.

How can I explain to her my obsession with Chinatown, with the vernal explosion of seeping color that is poetry there, the seesaw riddles, the dim sum that makes you go quack, and the expensive porcelain that glitters in the pale moonlight? The outrageously dutiful Ming hats with the little *ding* buttons on the top, the dim frogs with the Chinese coins in the tongues that make you *gaga*?

Like a Sino freak that is out of control, I hop in my car and pump the gas and make way for the heavenly gateway. With the coin in my pocket, I pray to the Buddha and feel the synergy of the highways, press the gas pedal, and forge ahead. Like some wayfarer of the clouds of a seeker of the Tao, I'm eager to dig into the fortress of the supernatural. With a light touch of the cool breezes, I'm sailing into space toward the land of the monkeys.

***

As I shudder inwardly and finger my *lucky me* coin, I'm not sure whether to feel truly inspired by the shaman or repulsed by him; only God knows. With the loud brass gongs clashing all about my ears like gun smoke, I run out past the brambleberry patch, thinking surreal thoughts about the universe and time and everything. Monkey-town, with its clownish antics and enlightened humor, with its glossy plentiful jades and distilled pewter fog, begins to haunt me like a conger chasing me through the thrill of the night. When I reach Master Charlie's, a costume shop on Polk Street, an old building painted waxy yellow, which is beat up in a sinister fashion, I rap on the front door three times and wait. A gnarly old man with a face as dour as birch wood suddenly answers and opens it up.

I walk in and survey the place; I discover it's a huge colonial house which resembles a high-life museum dating back to the 1920s, with Rhenish mannequins everywhere dressed in Ming Dynasty garb, flashy grape-colored silks that grab your squid eye, monocles which morph like black-headed beetles. Women in flaming red embroidered gowns on models with solemn alabaster faces, fragrant stitch in forgotten time. Shuffling about from room to room, I see, sitting in the back of the house, a tiny spittoon against the canonical wall, taking me wholly by surprise.

I reach inside my inner pocket, pull out the special coin, and toss it in, hearing it clink literally inside the spittoon, and an insular voice say "gotcha!" in my ears. Some misfit sound of the old theater era, charming me to the hilt.

Two minutes later, the sweet sound of oriental music from a brocade zither bursts throughout the entire house, as the wall besides the spittoon revolves quickly, turning; and I find myself in another stinking room, a red-paneled codicil with a cushioned leather couch where I'm sitting face to face with an stingy-faced woman that appears to be a quaint, old-fashioned gypsy, with a blue turban on her swollen bee head. With her frothy seaside manner, her round ivory face wavering in the sylvan April winds and her fragile, unkempt smile, her bouffantlike strands of perfumed glory, and her laughing wicker teeth brushed fastidiously so as to be so vanilla white. Her penitent arch brow was penciled in with a pat dark brown that was an eerie, desperate glow.

In her pale withered hands was a jade crystal ball, two full feet in free diameter, that glimmered like an ape's skull. She smelled of smelt lilac and silvery moth balls and had an itsy-bitsy spider in her busaceye and laughed grandiloquently off-key. What I remember of her was her tattered blouse the color of bloody persimmons and her stubby chin, which was covered with sugary hairs as if to suggest an expensive bonsai.

"So I see the shaman sent you?" she said, cackling at a high soprano pitch shrilly, doing some Toisanese incantation of the holy dead. So duly exotic were her warring chants, which were a smack of moonlit verbiage and slang, I became at once disarmed, immediately falling under her fairy-tale spell and beguiled by her every word. Her language ancient as the burning seaside and as whimsical as the floral spray in her teeth, her nose as pointed as a winced rose just fretted for eternity. What can I say to her, of my travails, of my famished heart, of my on-the-spur travels to Chinatown to this frail parlor creature who cares nothing about the future and the past to be sure?

"I see you well that you have a future and a past that comes together like a sampan boat smashing into the waters!"

"You don't know anything about me!" I say back with a vehement huff, looking cheeky.

"I'm not so sure about that—why do you come to Chinatown?" she asks with wizened eyes that abuse me.

"Don't ask—you ask too many questions," I rebuke, laughing a bit rebelliously, much to my surprise.

"I can tell you have a past that needs telling," she says, cackling, motioning to the huge crystal ball, dancing about until her lash hair grows darker.

"Don't tell me about the past—I know about all that," I say curtly back to her, admiring her a bit.

"Tsk, tsk . . .," she says, rubbing the crystal ball, quickly motioning her hands.

"How about these photos?" she says suddenly, pulling out some black-and-white pictures and putting them in front of me. "What do you think of these?"

As I'm about to answer her, I look at the dog-eared photographs under the frazzled light and am shocked to see glamorous Kodak pictures of my mother as a young vivacious woman, a seductress kissing another Chinese man who is not my father. In the photo, she looks glamorous and kitschy, wearing a pink check kerchief, a white A-line strapless dress that is off-fitting and entirely miffs the naked eye.

"What do you think?" asks the gypsy, looking at once buzzed out and egregious. "Gotcha!" she hisses. "How much will you pay for these photographs?"

I stutter and say nothing at all and look absolutely shocked and, upon closer examination, recognize the man in the photo as Mr. Yee. It's all so outlandish that I then run out the door, with the gypsy trailing me with her arms flailing in the air, screaming, "If you ever want to know any more . . ."

***

"What do you want me to say?" my mother, who is as old as layered, jaded wallpaper, asks later as she sits in her dusty apartment, shaking uncomfortably with a cough, smoking her studded Marlboros. Her happy eyes are peeled wide open as the ancient, reverberating waves of the sea, and the room smells like Tiger Balm and moth balls, of water chestnuts and frying-grease, so pungent, that that it makes my nostrils twitch.

"So you had an affair with Mr. Yee when you were only nineteen, and you never told anyone about this?"

"Why so much to tell? I was only a young girl living on Jackson Street. Up to no good. It was before I met your dad who was a doctor."

"Did you love him? How long did it last?"

"Hmmm . . . I can't remember," she says, looking somewhat embarrassed to be herself, her gray hair piled up upon her head like many layered sand way goose rings. I try to picture her and Mr. Yee together as a couple and can't believe it myself, my mother, of all people, going out with the mai tai man down the street.

"Was he handsome? He's nothing but an old bum now!"

"He was one of the most attractive men in Chinatown!" she snaps back at me and then softens, laughing. "I really didn't know any better."

"Why, of all people, Mr. Yee? What was so special about him?"

"Of course, I love your dad more, but for a while, about a summer, Mr. Oswald Yee was all the world to me!" she confesses and looks into the distance with a dreamy, unkempt stare. Her wrinkled, no-nonsense hose crinkles up, her many tox gold rings glistening with a succulence of the times, and there was a simpering in her voice that sounded like whammy-up insolence.

"He's not that great, of course, but once, we went to the Hotel L'Orange . . ."

Her voice cuts off then, and she shudders, looking a mite off-color, and stammers something incomprehensible at that. "Such a romantic night, only to be followed by . . . something unforeseeable!"

As her cloudy brown eyes mist over suddenly, she gets up slowly and walks over to her wooden dresser and pulls out a piece of certificate paper that is bent over in half and covered with thick wormy dust and looks at it drily with a quizzical stare. As she unfolds it, she reads it over with a horrified eye and says, "I never told your father, but look at this. I didn't get an abortion."

On the paper, a birth certificate, fading in blue streamline colors, reads the name "Alicia Yee, born to Jane Wu."

"What happened to the baby?" I ask her, looking visibly shocked.

"We gave her away to the Wing family. They had no children of their own and were willing to take her in. And that's all I know!" she said with a leftover tear in her eye, hugging the certificate, nuzzled to her breast.

"You know, Ma, I never realized there were all these dark secrets about you!" I say, hugging her close.

"It's been years and years. I could never tell your father the truth, or anyone else. How did you find out? Did Mr. Yee tell you?"

I laugh again and say that it was just some little bird that whispered in my ear, that secrets will divulge themselves in Chinatown, like some illicit chapter unspoken. "It's a strange world," I hiss to myself as I let myself out the door after comforting my mother and assuring her that everything is A-OK. As I crawl into my Volvo and drive away, I see an image of an innocent young woman, supposedly named Alicia Yee, calling out my very name.

"Everything is everything. Life is strange!" says the shaman, appearing in my cast-off oblivion dreams, praying in a floating pile of cumulus clouds. I shudder and stare at the hexagonal ba gua windows on the walls of my apartment and wait for tomorrow and the next day after, dreaming all through the night about Chinatown and its obtuse grimming lights.

***

Over sunny-side up eggs and a penitent rose ooze of ketchup and some daub of milk tea at Wally's on Fifth Street the next morning, I appear at once bleary-eyed, with suspense, dreaming of my half sister, wondering who she could be. *Alicia Yee.* The eponymous name sounds rooted with deep apoplexy, and as I inquire at the counter to see if anyone's ever heard of such a person, I'm disappointed by a definitive answer of no. *It's possible that she moved away,* I think quietly to myself, but perhaps the Wing family might know something of the other.

As I'm reading the paper, cutting my rough belvedere toast in two and spreading out my sliver of jam, I hear the sound of hard aping knuckles rapping on the table with censorious laughter, only to look up and see Mr. Fong wearing a simple gown with loud corn-colored teeth. In his rotten lapel, pinned is a white flower calyx which contorts. Outside, I can hear the obnoxious brassy horns of the funeral procession, which causes me to suddenly spill a splotch of runny egg yolk on my shirt.

Like some *basso profundo* horns tooting the end of a fine beat era, the funeral songs of those Chinatown coffins passing by in the superlative crowd are covered in a layered parfait confetti, the face of a dead corpse of a twisted vampire queen mouth not quite done with her palaver, her flash diamonds and tiara worn just right under the quondam light, the celebratory music of the people dancing right through her paltry skeleton. It is the mystery of her haunting figure that scares me, her tawdry lashes that are covered with garish makeup that still keeps me on my rancid toes, writhing in the heat, beating down on the pavement of inner Chinatown searching for an uncertain love. The lulled quiet of the full moon and its *huzza-huzza* surrounds the parceled city like an anxious searchlight, and there is longing with outrageous gypsy shadows, the frank outburst of solvent tears, etc.

"That was Mrs. Wing, the owner of Paradise Bakery. Can you believe she was eighty-eight when she died of lung cancer?" says Mr. Fong, choking suddenly on a stiff elongated cigarette.

"The Wings?" I ask, sounding excited, pausing with a bit of hesitation. "Do you know if they have a daughter named Alicia?"

"They have many children. I'm not sure which one you're talking about," he said, coughing, looking suddenly worried. "Why do you ask, m' dear?"

"No reason," I say, unperturbed to say the least.

"You do sound very up-and-up in arms about something!" he says, looking a tad suspicious in the eye. His octagonal face then warps up like a haze of pale fire.

"I'm just curious. That's all," I say sarcastically, staring at my dry toast with a straight expression. I confess that I'm not sure where I've been or where it's at.

"Just watch your step, young lady—Chinatown is a no-man's town— one wrong step, and you're in the spider's lair!"

As Mr. Fong then spooks away in an incessant whorl of stingy smoke and a spigot of charmed rose, in a full-blown Confucian fantasy, I tremble and then see Ming, wearing his calculus of sea green bifocals, suddenly enter Wally's with a portfolio and a neat set of ink brushes tucked under his tender, calloused hands. As he sees me, he bows in his quaint, antediluvian way and then sits down and begins to make his famous grotto sketches, mimicking Tang artists of yore with a yawn and a pseudoblip in space.

"Old Mrs. Wing has suddenly died of lung cancer. What do think of it?" I ask him, looking up from the dining table. His expression, his humorless, and his wryness, like the texture of old varmints in the movies.

"Think of it? Why, today is a day of celebration, for my dearest Alicia will be set free from her curse. I'm wearing a bright red ribbon around my dark head for joy," he says, pointing to the floral ring of roses around his neck.

"You know Alicia Yee?" I ask, brimming with outright curiosity and joy.

"Alicia *Wing*, the youngest daughter and the prettiest one, starved in the kitchen and ill treated for years by that no-good stepmother of hers!"

"What's she like?"

"The most beautiful, darling thing you can imagine who beats her brains in the bakery and goes out at night to get the men to feed herself. That curse of primal Chinatown in her! I tell her I love her, but she doesn't care!"

"You mean she's a prostitute!"

"Call it what you want. Now the old bitch has left her a hundred thousand bucks, and she's golden. Yes, today's a day for rejoicing!"

I cried inwardly to hear such a story and threw up my fists at old Mrs. Wing, the woman in the coffin who just passed by, shuddering to hear the lousy fate of my sister Alicia, given away, only to live a fate of the wastrel in the bakery of the damned, only to be delivered by the death of the famous bakery witch of Chinatown. How could I tell my mother who lived in fear of repercussions of the worst kind?

"Where do the Wings live?"

"On Hamoth and Sixteenth, on the red brick. Alicia's in the bakery right now on Polk Street. Why in the world do you ask?" His entire face looks rudely shocked lit up by pure indignation.

"No reason," I say to Ming, looking verily embarrassed. "It's just that I have an urgent message to deliver to her."

"She's cleaning her things out of the bakery and about to move to a better, safer place. You can catch her there."

"When the old lady died, did she say anything?" I asked nervously.

"One word, about the money, just take it all," said Ming with a droll, uncouth laugh as he began to do his *mao-bi* or brush strokes again. He had a serious fairy tooth glint in his eye and was looking at a book full of foodle diagrams that looked cryptic, full of snakes and trip ladders.

I then left Wally's with a sentimental tear in my eye and a cynical shudder in my breast, full of dread for the outgoing karma of Monkey-town, as much as I welcomed it in the beginning, thinking of the bouts of gunshot and cancer, of the bad stinging stories of heartache I heard as a child, the tragic, lefstry in the making. The wellspring rain bursts through the doors and leaves me covered in a thick piñata soot, wandering in a trance, leaving me almost wishing I'd never come.

****

I glared at the shaman for a moment and wondered what he knew of kingpin Chinatown and its thrice-colored birdcages, its easterly winds, and its blitzkrieg of occasional lights. What sweet words of salvation he would find in his ladle from the congee blaster and how he preached with such devotion to the dreamy-eyed masses.

"I give you my streetwise words, my lamp-lit babies to cry with," he confessed with a bit of a blue lip. "Monkey-town is not that deep . . . It's just about counting the beads in the runnels of your hem." He let out huskily, looking warily nervous.

As I leave him behind in the Pentecostal fog, he waves good-bye and wishes me good luck as I then rush over to Paradise Bakery, entertaining outlandish thoughts of Monkey-town and of the shaman and his earthbound Shambhala. What could the fluted words of the gypsy mean, and what else could that earthling know? As I open the ramshackle doors, I rush inside with rabid disorder in my heart, and I suddenly see a strange-looking young woman with engaging flashing eyes polishing a dish look directly at me with an accusing glance.

"If it's desserts you want, the bakery's closed," she says with a drawn-out yawn and looks at me with a phlegmatic smile.

"I'm actually not here for the food. My name's Jenna," I say with an awkward pause, not sure what to say at first. "I'm your half sister," I blurt out like a fool outright. "Your mother, Jane, told me to find you after all these years. We didn't know you were here!"

"That's nice, but you seem to be out of your mind. My mother died a long time ago. I'm just a brat from Jackson Street."

"I'm sorry—she actually gave you away at birth because there was nothing else she could do! I heard the Wings treated you horribly!"

"What's this about? Some sad soap opera? The old Wing lady is dead—some carcass in the mud—I should say I'm going to rejoice! What's your name again?"

For a while, she looks startled, annoyed, and then giggles at a high-stumbling pitch and reaches in her purse for a tiny note card to give me.

"Look, Jenna, I don't have time for all this crap. But Ming and I are getting married tonight for sure. Why don't you come by for the ceremonies at Lucky Peach on Polk Street? There will be a lot of people there. And say hi to your mom. Or my mom. Whatever."

And with a manic giggle, she walks away behind the dark bakery curtain, humming some opera lines from *Phantom,* waving good-bye.

"Was the old Wing lady that mean to you?" I ask plaintively with tears in my eyes.

"Sometimes," she said in a cold voice, back coldly, "but what can you expect from those losers? They're toast in the brains!"

As I rush away, I think upon the skein of Monkey-town and look at the invitation card, which says *Momofuku,* Lucky Peach, and bless my half sister and Ming. The entire city is so full of wizards and temptress, full of hard knocks and bless-outs, like half lanterns hanging from a slew of electric-colored strings.

I curse the Wings and walk on past Geary and all that clattering traffic until I run into Mrs. Wong who is rushing eagerly to see me in her parlor-print dress, her uppity curls, and her angelic nose. She is running up to me, her arms full of vegetables and soppy tea bags, looking at me with an accusing glance.

****

"Now don't you dare go to Lucky Peach tonight," says Mrs. Wong with a strikeout, her arms flailing in the air like a real brutal matron of the times. "Alicia is nothing but a common hussy, and all her vampish friends will be there, a real mockery of the word *marriage* or double happiness. I protest this! There's nothing lucky about this. Ming is crazy, crazy as a loon!"

"What's wrong with it?" I demand, showing her my mucked-up invitation. "Alicia has had a hard life and is my half sister. Why *not* go? You have such a hard heart."

"You young people just don't understand the traditions. Ming should be married to a real woman of the city, not some floozie with a bow in her hands, even if she has a million bucks! What sense is there in it? These people are crazy!"

"You're just too mean," I protest. "Alicia is so wonderful—has spent her whole life serving the Wings. Now that she has her freedom, she should be happy! Why not give her a break?"

"See it your way—I'm just warning you of the worst. You people who don't follow the traditions, will break hearts, and see gloom and doom."

"I'm sorry you see it that way, Mrs. Wong, but I respect your views nonetheless!"

As a hemo-winged pigeon flies off the gilded rooftops of one of the buildings of Jackson Street, Mrs. Wong hurries off to protest the wedding with her bouncy curls in a druthers, her heels in burning smoke. I cursed her zealotry and tried to remain calm and decided to head for Felicia's to look for something suitable to wear for the wedding ceremonies, perhaps a *chongsam* or a long dress with chit heels.

I then begin to imagine all the hoopla at Lucky Peach, all the daring comments that will be made and dismiss it as sheer nonsense. As the gossip flew throughout the city, I could see doors opening and closing, lots of wild Cantonese tongues snapping frostily throughout the day in support of Old Lady Wing who was so femme brutal. Like a praying mantis with an elegant *tsing*, the young people who support Alicia fly out of their houses, singing her praises, fighting back the whole rainbow city in a rambunctious uproar.

****

Heading out to Sammy's, I walk past the blooming yew trees which blow this and that way, hearing the crackling firecrackers pop like hot fire in the far distance. Ahead in the freesia shadows is the shaman in his trendy patchwork coat, lighting up a slim cigarette with both trembling hands, his tousle of moplike hair standing out like an awesome aureole.

"So you've come into the magical city and found that the city is in your blood, my friend!" he says, patting me on the back. His teeth, which are shock-white, look like alligator's klebanger, sharp and alarmingly dashing.

"That's true, Master Shaman, that's true," I laugh, flirting with him.

"What do you think of our Alicia?" he asks, his mournful eyes full of tinted compassion.

"I'm not sure," I admit breathlessly. "She's getting married tonight!"

"That's true! Be there at the Lucky Peach Restaurant. And be sure to be there on time!"

And with an elegant snap of his slender thumbs, he departs, like a hopeless revenant heading out toward Waverly Place, a drunken hyena among the mystic clouds, his eyes burning like ingots in the sky. I decide to run after him, intoxicated in the heat, but then stop myself and continue to head over to Sammy's where I can see Mr. Yee sitting at the counter, looking surprised and thoroughly delighted in the robust tan face.

"So you talked to her?" he says with a wide smile that disarms me.

"Of course I did," I say back, twittering.

"And you'll be at Lucky Peach tonight?" he says, tapping his fingers on the counter.

"Yes, as I surely promised I would be."

"You know, I could never do much for her, but at least now she's her own person. That Wing Lady was just the pits!"

As I hug him and sigh, walking around the store, it's then that I feel instantly related to everything in the realm of Monkey-town and all the people in it, as if the gigantic frothy cosmos were moving in that particular direction. *Lucky Peach it is,* I think to myself. As I survey all the shelves, I find the crystal turtle vase I had been eyeing for weeks and take it to the front desk only to hear Mr. Yee say, "I say for free. It's a gift from me as well. How about that?"

"Are you sure? I can pay. It's no big deal."

"I say for free."

With many tears in my eyes, I say thank-you to Mr. Yee, looking at his face to get a glimpse of his slanted holy eyes and run out the store, breathing in the dappled sunlight. With my head in the clouds and my tiny heart beating fast, I head back to Jackson Street where I see the hobnob peddlers chisel the newbie names of children on little pieces of pale rice. It's a marvelous day in Monkey-town where the kaleidoscope lives of beautiful people thrum together like Lego or buildings blocks of colorful stripes and erstwhile polka dots.

I slowly hum some song from a live game show and keep moving like an earthy robot, digging my feet into the sidewalks of suburban pleasure, some ticktock limbs in me, allowing me to breathe again after so much unceasing nervous anxiety.

***

Later that night, inside Lucky Peach, the evening crowd cawed about the restaurant and took pictures of Alicia and Ming who are dressed up to the nines, infancy red velveteen garb, standing in front of a six-foot peach-blossom tree and a triple-layered fondue cake. There were traditional firecrackers in the air, crackling like the sizzling sound of electric g-wires and the many funny-faced guests saunter about making outlandish, whiplash comments about how stunning and eerily gorgeous the bride is.

"Guess what she wore?" hissed one guttersnipe, Old Mrs. Lin, the seamstress from Polk Street with a lofty weathered brow. "The most expensive *chongsam* from the Shanghai . . . to think of it!" Amid much sneering and ballyhoo of streetwise gossip, Ming kisses his bride as the rude guests clink their generous glasses of wine, toasting to the future of Chinatown at large, simpering all the while.

"You'll see that Mrs. Wong was all wrong!" snaps Mr. Fong in his best green fedora, clapping his dark hands to the *pipa* music in the background, doing the twist and turn, and saluting Alicia in a loud, aping voice, which warms her simple heart. "She looks just so charming, and Ming is so damned wonderful—what a pair!"

"That's right, Mr. Fong—a toast to the two of them!"

Among the guests are Mr. Wu, the seedy watermelon peddler from Waverly Place from Hong Kong, and Ms. Chew, the big tycoon's daughter from Macau who flirted shamelessly with all the guests with a low-cut bodice dress which scared everyone. Also present were Mrs. Bong, the owner of Jing Jing Supplies from Wing Street, and Mr. Cho, the owner of the fortune cookie factory on Jackson Street who was leading the entire fray with suspicious wavy eyes which flattered like diamonds.

The light-shattering jade drapes in the restaurant glistened beside the double happiness sign as Ming and Alicia paraded about, clinking their sparkling champagne, much to the loud applause and some crude sniping from the audience that clamored away like a crowd of brick brats with vicious forked tongues.

"I've never seen such a thing," whispered Ms. Chew to Mr. Low of Ng's Shipping Company who had glittering snake eyes that miffed; the two were having an affair and were said to be seen together in the city often drinking mai tai on and off. "It's like something on a reality show," he let out with a droll purlieu, looking drunk indeed.

"Why don't you shut up, you hussy!" said Mrs. Yang who sat at the next table and didn't take well to Ms. Chew's off-color adventitious overtures. They had once been mah-jongg buddies but had separated after a nasty brouhaha over who had better horoscopes, better health, and more attractive, outgoing children. Glaring at each other in the blinking C-light, they exuded a deathly touch of sinister competition that dangerous misfit Chinese women are so wont to have in these times.

Mr. Fong walked up to the front of the stage and toasted the two, singing a few saintly bars from "Peach Blossom Orchard" under his abated breath, and bowed low to a saunter of a haunting trill. "We here in Monkey-town salute Ming and Alicia." The two kissed under the twinkling double happiness sign and sat down and cut the gigantic cake as everyone applauded, except for Ms. Chew who snickered rather loudly, much to everyone's aghast.

"What's that with you, Ms. Chew?" said Mr. Fong who eyed her then with wild eyes and knew she had been a close friend of the old Mrs. Wing when the old harpy had been alive. "Why can't you be happy for Alicia, young lady?"

"It's nothing—don't bother me—it's just some tear in my eye! To think it, that she's getting married after all she's done!"

"*Bot por—why don't you be quiet?*"

And with sharp rebuff, Mr. Fong waved her away quickly with his leathery hands and sat down with an angry, silly-sally grin on his face and drank his mai tai, his inky spidery hands showing deep splotches of blue stinky futch. The double dragons on the shylo curtains began to simper with insistent glee, and all the entire crowd waxed hypnotic as they make lofty predictions about the coming year, about the solid prices of the fish on the table, about who will make good in the proper business, and about who will be the next bride.

****

PART II

LUCK MING

Out of the deeps of Frisco, the wildflowers bloom contemptuously, leaving dust for thought and sparkles of lost energy in the air. There are some supernatural elements to this little enclave called Chinatown, where flora and fauna are entwined with the threnody of spring, and sweet memories of the years flood the eyes, like the gorgeous lazy-eyed susans and asyminthys which dot the gardens of the old harpy women who mill about, garnering sunlight under their hats. It was on a severe lucky day that I chanced upon old Mrs. Tang in the nursery where she was measuring her steps with dolorous eyes of doubt and suspicion.

"That's deep, so you've come for your horoscope," said the old potter who sat in her backyard at Waverly Place under the tall ecru sunflowers and looked at my small hand, tracing the wavy lines, much to my acute, discordant displeasure. "So it's Monkey-town you love. And you've even found a half sister! Hmph."

"What's this about? A gypsy?"

"I'm not sure," I answer, looking absurdly scared. "These things in Monkey-town are wild and very superbly cosmic. Out of this raging world."

"Have you tried looking at your astrology signs? You're a Gemini, I see that."

"That's true—I'm a double-headed giant—very stubborn to a hilt."

"What I see in the future for you is genius—and a very special brew of tea. Do you like white tea, darling?"

"I drink any sort of tea. Lipton is fine for me."

"Not Lipton. That's American tea. I mean white tea or oolong tea. Something that will give you deep cloud breath. Change your fortunes. Make your mind float forward."

"Anything to change my luck I'll try . . ."

"Why don't you go to Jade Palace, and order this . . .," says old Mrs. Tang with a wry, spouting face, writing up some list of characters in bold clear Chinese for me on a small crumpled piece of white paper. "Say then I sent you!"

As I then thank her, she goes back to shoveling the pace dirt around her tall, abstruse bending sunflowers under her wide-brimmed cornflower hat and smiling her brown-faced Cantonese smile, which touches me. Hunched over in her purple-faded chemise, which fits loosely, she looks just like my grandmother, toothy and winsome and able to see the future as it were, a smidgen of a visionary chimera on her hairy lips. I thought and dreamt that she could touch the *seema* of dragons in the clouds, a thimble of arcane wisdom in her breast, the ken of ultimate desire that makes Monkey-town bend at her every sacred whim. What makes it tick and tock is this ensemble of golden outrageous metaphors that is the sassy den south of San Francisco, the Buddha's green thumb that makes supernatural crickets sing again.

****

Two days later, at the wide doors of Jade Palace, I nervously hand the waitress my crumpled slip of paper, and she serves me a mysterious dish of red bean soup in a miniature steaming porcelain tea bowl covered with leafy white fungus and cloud shitake mushroom wood ears, a traditional dish so lofty in presence that I'm not sure what to make of it at first.

"Are you sure this is it?" I asked, a little put off by the woodsy, odiferous smell, which made me want to faint straight away with a whist and a clamor.

"That's what it says," said the waitress, chortling quizzically and waltzing out the back door with ritzy, glam eyes.

As I poke my fork into the odd confection and begin to dig in, I dream of far-off lands like Shangri-la and try my luck with the cloudy fungus, which makes my perm frizz out. Halfway into this so-called dessert, my fork rips into a piece of tag paper at the bottom of the dish, a scrap note in vivacious red ink which reads, "Meet me at ABC Funhouse at noon. Important news. –Mr. Fong." Startled to see his handwriting in such elaborate flurries and impresario loop de loops, I see the cool thingamajig in my food staring out at me like a fancy spacey anagram of the first order.

Pushing the rest of the half-eaten fungus away from me and exiting quickly out the restaurant, I head down Geary Street past the plum-colored edifices, which shimmer in arcadian light, and show me the way like some twinkling billboard of letters. As I trample the sylvan grass with my feet, I saunter past the foliage toward the famous international burger joint, periodically checking my watch whose bling numbers swing a quarter till noon, much to my relieved, full-blown anxiety.

As I arrive, I walk quickly inside, only to see the notorious Mr. Fong sitting there wearing his silly simple corn silk smile and wearing his best suit, holding blooming flowers, the startling color of severe opium smoke.

"What's up, Mr. Fong?" I suddenly said, growling with deep curiosity.

"I need your help, Jenna—it's the passion of passions!" he says with a tear in his eye.

"Whose the flower for, old man?"

"It's for that Flora, the new woman from Hong Kong who works at the flower shop," he says, goofing in his powdery, ginseng voice; his chirpy, round face crackles with acute, syncopated pleasure. Some metered ounce of gravitas in his leathery skin glisten with precious moonbeam in the constellations.

"What's the problem—why did you send for me?" I ask with a bemused voice, so happy to see the old alligator man passionately in the throes of love at last.

"I'm not good enough—an old scanty man like me with scabrous coolie skin and an old jack-o'-lantern face! How can I become fashionably handsome again? You can teach me the tricks, Jenna! I've heard that you did beauty school!"

"I'm not sure what you're talking about, Mr. Fong. I'm not *that* smart, but I can help get you dressed up like a shocka. In return, how about you get me free lunch at Yeo's sometime?"

"It's a deal—now what's the first lesson in graces?"

"It's to buy some real aftershave—and stop wearing that awful mothball stuff—it's grotesque!" I say, a bit in a confessional tone.

"Should I get a tattoo that says 'I love you, monkey'?"

"Stop kidding around, Mr. Fong, or you'll never impress her!"

"Okey dokey!"

"When's your first date, sir?"

"Next Tuesday, at Venus Café. I'm ordering the clams with the linguine! Sur le tat!"

"Why not we go Alberto's to pick out a new suit for you? That gig will make you stunning as *Leave It to Beaver!*"

"To Alberto's it is!"

As he cracks his vivacious knuckles and sucks his grim fossil teeth, Mr. Fong brushes back his enduring flush of gray hair and lets out an innocent Bauhaus laugh and speaks of his new love interest, a stunning parlor maid from Hong Kong who has wavy, undulant hips and slapdash ruby eyes to match. He is all pleasantries and tomfoolery, a Popeye the Sailor type who knows Monkey-town front to back and speaks the old Toisanese dialect with a distinct peppery brogue of sorts. What makes his hairy tongue tick and his wide animé eye glisten with oily shine is the fob watch in his velveteen pocket, that surreal catch of numbers, his onerous burden of juicy words crystallizing like true spit on the snatch. I salute him just as the shade cuts across his brow, leaving him breathless and truly unaccountable like those wisps of the planet Mars who are hidden from the moon. Just like those fortunates who never wander far from the spigot or the spout.

***

Any fine bloke could outdo old Mr. Fong in pompous antics were it not for his likable gumshoe poetics, his rubber-ducky tummy, and his quick-shine moustaches which glow like the Mohabie dessert in the vast array of keen proper effects in the coming. As he torched himself in the vain outdoings of a Romeo of the new century, we learned to love this, some old passions of the modern heart. It was his ticktock fantasy to suit up with kind flair so as to seduce his Madonna, his Flora-on-the-go. How could I, a simple valley girl with a panache for helping lost itinerant souls, do anything else but help him out by taking him to Alberto's, an outfit that I'm sure you'll agree has all the starch of a vain apple on the studs? It was that simpleness of his cupie heart which moved me, made the Cantonese gal in me driven to distraction and tears, some purple stripe of the good country.

At Alberto's, a little men's tailor store on Polk Street, which is packed with outrageous cello-colored suits and bindi-colored ties, a natty short man named Mr. Louie sorts his wedged green bills with orange half spectacles and measures dolorous cloth with a hideous fat thumb, combing his comb with absolution. "How dashing and eccentric the people are who come here," he says with splashy pride in his *basso profundo* voice, walking up and down the wooden one-two step ladder in the room and putting on sycophantic petty airs.

Mr. Louie is an arrogant man who despises the shaman and his superstitious lingo, his ongoing pitch of the celestial stars that makes all the other people in the city shudder completely.

"To think it, that these people don't believe in common sense and science!" he kvetches rather boldly, looking with a tyrannical face at the horoscope calendar. "Of course they believe in the shaman—they're all a bunch of busybodies!"

"Oh—you're so mean," says Mrs. Louie, a spindly faced woman who is counting her tunable jade rosary on a finger and praying for better health. "Why mock the shaman? He is a wonderful man! A saintly man!"

"Pooh-pooh on that! He's nothing but an impostor! To hell with him!"

As the many courtly people of Chinatown come and go in the store, some children make fun of Mr. Louie's large belly, calling him none other than the famous balloon man, yelling sharp invectives in rude Cantonese that make him turn bright alien blue. *"Say-pot-gay!"* he yells back to a young child on the block outside his store who is sticking a middle finger up at him.

All over the city, there is the slight touch of impersonation of a grist like a dowager's thread pulled too tight, a brocade of flashy border's tears, glistened solid gold with vivid tangerine sparks. The young cassia trees glisten with their unkempt leaves all over the place in a fixed pool of radar light in the sun. The young hoods leave their slim cigarettes in the dirt, as it to signify some rather Buddha touch and the singular beat of the fractured ego continues, as if on cue, like a vain jukebox in full continuous play.

As Mr. Fong and I enter into Alberto's, it's as if we are entering another juicy portal, like an *Archie* comic book strip. The falling yucca tree leaves curl up like morphed kitten tails and the motes of sunshine flood the shop, lighting up each tailored suit like a foolish rave body. The derby hats look super keen, and the glossy ties glisten like a parfait scoop, like wild duck tongues speaking the language of despair.

"If it isn't the elegant Mr. Fong!" exclaims an excited Mr. Louie, running out to meet him with thick outstretched hands with grotesque fingers.

"That's right, Mr. Louie. I'm here to be suited up! And looking my best," he says with a waxy grin that stretches from side to side.

Smiling my best, I offer my hand to Mr. Louie and say I'm new to this bum-out called Monkey-town, an outsider just learning new ropes but happy to see his shop of mystical horrors. "So truly wonderful to meet you," I present myself with a nervous tic, chortling at the top of my celebratory lungs.

"What will it be today? A lavender tie with a blue serge suit might look good on you, old Joe!"

"Lavender is too feminine for me. How about hot red?"

"Red it is, Fred."

"And how about that bowler hat for fifty bucks?"

"Sold to you, Joe!"

As they chat greedily, I walk around Mr. Louie's shop from front to back and see Mrs. Louie sitting in the back room, the lauding shadow of her praying, saying her Hail Marys. As I'm about to leave, it's her trembling voice I hear calling me.

"Who are you?"

"I'm Jenna, the friend of Mr. Fong."

"Oh, I'd like to hi to you and ask you to say hi to the shaman for me!"

And with a sharp whimper and a hiss, she hands me her ace rosary, with a chubby round hand, the picture of her pale, obese face in tears.

"What's the matter?" I ask, fretfully.

"Oh, it's nothing—just moved by all he has to say!" she says, whispering in a voice that scares me. "He moves mountains like a flying dragon from the skies!"

As I say my last good-bye, I look closely at her vision in the waning light only to see a black-ringed eye over her rounded cheeks above a sprinkling of traumatic tears. Like a hobbit's wife, she continues to pray viciously in the dark and wait patiently for the shaman's enlightened lectures.

As I saunter out the entrance of the front adjoining door, I nod to Mr. Fong who is all dressed up and looks like a frank-spoken czar in vermillion threads; some elegant intruder is the mist.

"What do you think?" he opines, grinning naughtily like a spacey nutcracker from front to back, turning around and around with a twixel. "Do you think my Flora will go nuts?"

"You look great, Mr. Fong. Now let's get outta here. It's giving me the creeps."

I shudder inwardly and quickly finger the rosary in my purse and pray that I'll see the shaman again soon, if at all, to be honest. In Monkey-town, there are monkey eyes and flaming dinosaur tattoos everywhere, superbats that fly through the glassed window shades and greasy slips of paper that make you laugh with mist-laden messages in them. Like stories of wispy denouement, the world of subterfuge spins faster than your reincarnation, and you're left standing in its Diablo, a trapped puppet of no-good sorts left to fend for yourself. Stranger than its accord, it leaves you in a state of heavenly trance.

****

In Waverly Place, I'm told, where the glimmer of sere leaves blooms with a purling gold effect and the Aphrodite fish swim lovingly in the fish bowls, Flora Chew walks about in Chew's Floral Arrangements, biting her tapered nails, chipping off the lacquer bit by bit, her expensive coiffure a tad off. Her melancholic angel face is slender, and she slopes a bind, dreaming of the passing time, her dark knit dress just an inch hitch about her tender pelican knees which knock together. How shapely are her tweezed eyebrows and pouty her lips. How trilling her party-line Cantonese!

"These gerbera daisies are *weird*," she thinks mournfully to herself, just like her mussed-up stringy hair, and sprinkles water on them to see them garner light in the emblazoned store window where the seersucker sun makes the whole arrangement sparkle like chitsy. The drooping roses look somewhat amorous and fickle, and the daisies are charming to a hilt, each to each a splendid fragment of the frothy cosmos, a myriad shade that is alarmingly feminine.

"These alligator matrons don't want flowers. They want Coach purses!" screams Eliza, Flora's helper, a vivacious young woman in her late twenties who has been working there for over a year now. "Why so fancy? These horrendous flowers will never sell!"

"That's not true. Where's your imagination? Every dragon lady will want a purple lilac to put on her dressing table for the New Year!"

"It's up to you, Flora, but I'd rather have a kettle of fish."

Flora laughs wickedly and puts a vertiginous spin in her slim hips and walks around the room gazing at each flower and dreaming of Mr. Fong and giggles when she comes back to the gerbera daisy and repeats the word "weird" softly, kissing each lofty petal, thinking of him. *Why wait,* she thinks until he comes, *to put on her selvage makeup.* She puts on three coats of lipstick, kvetching in the mirror like an old witch up in arms.

"What are you doing?" asks Eliza who looks patently curious and puts down a stack of watery lilacs.

"Nothing . . . just wondering if I still have it," she says cynically, eyeing her lips with a stark shade of mauve with a sad tear in her eye.

"You look wonderful as always!" says Eliza. "You have a visitor at the front door."

With a slight twinkle of the miniature gold bell, the front door flies opens, and Mr. Fong steps in, wearing a shining black suit with a red tie, holding a Coach bag and gerbera daisies, screaming, "Gotcha!"

The double-dragon sash in the store glitters with manic stars, and all the outstanding flowers begin to bloom superfluously with a singular touch. The odiferous floral perfume of fresh flowers then suffuses the room, and Mr. Fong is left dancing in circle like a satyr on the go, his gimcrack mouth filled with wide, yaklike teeth.

"What do you think of these gerbera daisies?" he says naughtily. "I can read minds!"

Flora does a double-take and looks at Eliza suspiciously and twitters while the hydra of flowers bloom even more wildly, and she gives Mr. Fong her hand, and they walk out the door amid much hooting from the children on Jackson Street. As the two walk to the door, the heated orb of the sun sets, and the thick-haired matrons click their rowdy tongues and pour their tea from round clay bowls, exclaiming, "Never on Tuesdays but always on Wednesdays!"

***

Later on, at Tea Villa, the stench of oolong tea oozes in its shiny porcelain cups like some rotten elixir that tastes incredibly boorish, and the rice wafers leaf up high to the low ceiling above the greasy circle fan. The miniature cockroaches form an ensemble, lining up on the wooden tables, making their aubades with a careless whisper to the pock-faced sous-chef who resembles an old bagman smoking a cob pipe under some gold hinge roof of sorts.

"Make that two!" calls out the waiter to the sous-chef inside who is brewing all kinds of occluded anxiety leaves for the customers, dreaming of their saggy, pock-marked faces, their chattering tongues, and their juicy seasonal complexions. The crowded room is suffused with obnoxious chrysanthemum perfume, so aromatic that customers gasp and think of past ruinous dynasties, so scabrous that their midnight coiffure glimmer.

"That tea was pretty heavy—bring in the snuff powder!"

Amid quarreling tongues and blue tatami cushions where the customers sit cross-legged, sipping their cache of oolong, the aroma of udon wafts through the air and makes pretty hearts skip a beat. On the back walls are pictures of ancient Buddhas smiling from antiquity, a zither loom broken in two and some strained Tao creatures flying into deep space nine. Seated in the corner, sporting an old khaki army jacket, is the shaman, looking handsome as ever, drinking from a half-empty bamboo tea kettle covered with dust. He looks severely depressed and slightly drunk in the face to be sure.

"If it isn't you, I've been looking for you all over the place!" screams out Mrs. Wong as she bursts in the front door, her arms stuck straight up in the fresh air like ancient flypaper.

"What is it?" he says suddenly, drinking from his cup of tea, looking annoyed at once.

"You just don't know, but Ming is drinking again, and the whole marriage is turned topsy-turvy!"

"How do you know that, my dear Mrs. Wong?"

"Just something a little bird told in my ear!"

"What the hell do you want me to do about it?"

"Shake him out of the entire trance—and make him go home to his wife!"

"Where is he now?"

"At Snake Terrace—smoking by himself and haranguing with the bar women!"

"What's it about—always calling me at this hour?"

"Why, you're the shaman, of course!"

With two twitches of a thumb, the waitress brings the shaman his check, and he drinks up and smiles and gets up and shakes Mrs. Wong's groping hand and walks out the door guffawing loudly like a mighty dragon man. "Of course I'll help!" he offers loudly. "Old Ming is out of his mind!"

***

The rumble of a sweet peach in a wicker basket, phoenixes vanishing into the thrum of porcelain vanity cases. Some jig and jag, the flimflam from the South of China. These biblical revelations carved into the back of the mind like the *ticktock* of the ancient watch and the wild stork diving on a carved wooden plate. Some sampan trouble of the oceanic vault—two snatches of a thumb on an *er-hu*, a pictorial screen unfolding into a hidden anteroom with a zig and zag. The jaded dice tumbling out on the bamboo table, echoing the many high-pitched soprano voices on cue.

With his scotch of peanut-colored trousers rolled up to his bended knees and his Barney-styled hair soused halfway with fresh dandified liquor, Ming sits at a table drawing pictures of fraggled dinosaurs, crying out loud, unable to picture the flossy future, his shaded spectacles a spectacular mess. On the table are many piles of martini drinks and hors d'oeuvres that he can't finish up completely. Who is to fathom what is in his eccentric lock-stop brain, or why he can't draw his fancy diagrams or love Alicia anymore at that?

With many fresh tequilas arriving at the table on the cheap string and a damp inveterate spell of ghoulish piano music which made his ears leap, Snake Terrace was a portal of dreams for lost chaps in search of their furrowed brows and their naked hearts, a pit filled with human dishonor that made the soul run dry at the spigot. What awkward accordion playing there was, and what brassy horn busting! What flashy ace cards in the mix, and what intimate mah-jongg runs into the frosty dirt!

"You don't know—but you've been here for the last seventeen hours, Mr. Woo!" says the sultry waitress, teasing at him with open candor.

"I know, I know, but this drawing isn't finished yet! How about another drink?"

With a brow that grows thicker every second over his lovely Confucian eyes and beer stains that cover the rainy hem of his padded silk Confucian gown, Ming stutters over his drawings and stares dreamily into space, thinking of his wife, uttering mere nonsensicalities. His curvy lips are goose soul ether, and as he pens another drawing of the universe in startling strokes, tears fall, making the lines extremely blurry. How could his wife so cruel to him?

"Aw, Mr. Woo, why are you so sad? Your wife is a raving beauty! She is like the stars of Venus and sings like a peerless immortal! Why don't you go home?"

"That's true. She sings like a cockatoo in love with someone else!"

"You don't know, Mr. Woo, but you're a very drunken man!"

As the other bar drinkers toss their choice dice and drink their hot tequilas, old foodies with silk ties and florid smiles, he sees chancy lights of the city outside the oval window and cries, dreaming of the cold mercurial weather that breaks hearts. The daffodils bloom obstreperously with an infusion of color and fill the room with distinct perfume, and the crocodile smiles of the patrons allow his teeth to chatter wildly. What could he be possibly dreaming of, leaving his wife like that?

As the unbelievable purple smoke whorled into the room, the shaman busts in with an exquisite bunch of white roses in his hand and says, "Ming, what are you doing? Are you crazy?"

Ming cries and peers closely at his drawings and says nothing at first and glares at the shaman who looks at him with a surprised wry eye. "Why these drawings?" he says. "Why not at home with Alicia? The whole damned town is talking about you!"

"You know, you're silly, Ming. You're all about smoke and mirrors and the realm of Confucian studies. But what women like are roses. Why don't you bring her these petals?"

Ming sighs outright and pushes his spectacles up his handsome nose with a vehement huff and lets out a wild guffaw of exasperation. "Are you sure, Master Shaman? What's my predicted future?"

"What I see for you, my friend, is *bright, bright, bright* as the moon! Come here and feel this pale jade right here on my finger. What do you feel?"

"I feel absolutely nothing!"

"That's where you're wrong, my friend. You're feeling the cold beat of the deep eternity, the nexus of you and Alicia forever. It's in your lovely smile!"

"Are you sure?"

"I'm positive of it!"

"Why not go home, young soul?"

"Give me those roses, and it's a go!"

As the shaman quick furrows his brow and bows and gives him the roses, the whole crowd in the drunken golden palace applauds loudly, and Ming exits with tears in his dampened eyes. Just like that, a pithy ghost leaving in a puff of green smoke with courtly love on his dampened toes. Meanwhile in the room, a ditty for Cantonese matrons with smoke rings in their hair and white goose feathers in their hips, loud trombone playing in the streets where the city begins to muck it up with high flair. So much for the mayhem in the enlightened world of romp and dishonor, the treble clef of the dilettantes and the aficionados of the Tao.

****

A ladder of toss-away alphabet graffiti on Waverly Street all over the glittering garbage of the urban outlay, simple words of the outrageous monkey men in full bloom astound me, make me see cool Krishna blue at last. The castaway words of the city with its supple infinity and its double halo of feathers and smiles which echo quietly through sound waves of passing time. Fractured automobiles and leathered-up mutts moving down past the old yew trees and the stiletto of April shadows looking so distinctive in muffed-up suits. This last line of foul emperors in their fallen step, a corner for deep amour, the sweet taboo taste of the afterlife, the lucky coins of paradise in a round, large-size, *squeeze-me* piggy bank. All the trefoil leaves of the outré season tossing and turning on the cakewalk, tripling to be sure.

As Ming hurries back home in his silk-padded coat, his large catfish eyes sparkle with vim. He walks brusquely past Felicia's on Battery Street and walks inside, looking quite proud of himself. *You have that some wonderful imagination,* he thinks so profoundly and with eyes the expensive two-layered jade bracelet under the cheery glass window with a juicy squid pupil and says, "How much?"

"Fifty," the hoity-toity voice says back.

Ming then laughs and takes out his soiled bills and counts them one by one and makes the purchase and feels giddy inside. "That's that!" he says, feeling like high-time fountain paradise. If only he could buy the other fine jades, the stalling cockatoo made of precious red fountain ink jade and the tiny golden trinket elephant and put them in his pocket. These too would make wonderful presents!

"You know, Ming, you are only a beginning scholar, but someday your drawings will sell!" says the snobby lady in the window with a friendly smile. "Perhaps you can come back then and buy them all!"

"That's true, Mrs. Yu. That's true!"

With a stealthy wind in his autumn lung pipes, he begins to churn out a melody of five whistles and walks down the street dreaming of coy spiders and fry monkeys and feels duly charmed with the entire universe, albeit a many lump of coal in his chest. If only he could buy the rocking rooster with inkstone jade right now! His poised drawings were but frittle, but he treasured them and rolled them up under his bended arm and kept walking around about and about, left and right, ambling about as if he were some wind-up toy of the behemoth stars. *Why do that? Pursue the thoughts of the great masters if all you could buy was just one jade?* he thought.

The little shih tzu waved his measly paw to him and sighed, and the twisted honey tree blew to the left, and the whole street seemed empty. He looked at his handful of roses, and suddenly they didn't seem that wonderfully dear to him. He would never impress Alicia with just a two-tone jade bracelet that cost so little!

As he made his way past Waverly Street instead of bowing as he always did at the side street with a picture of the ba gua mirror and praying to the Tao, he cursed himself and thought some sinister thought and went the other direction instead of home. All he could see was the shaman's face screaming at him to be good.

****

At night, the subterranean fog casts the city in a pink vellum like a drape of stars; and in the bars, the Buddha-faced drinkers come out with scars on their fearless temples. With what temerity do they speak of their stories, and with what high-minded coven whispers do they cling to the present moment. What instigation there is in their loose banditry, and how they opine for a different style of casuistry where with crowlike hands they mutter lines from a Tang poem or brag of the victories of the day at Melbourne's Lucky Den? With the heady fish zither in their full plates, they dream of their afterlife and pray for the Tao. What gumption there is in their faces, and how they gamble for the future?

"This is my lucky dice!" says Mr. Ng, tossing up his dice in the gambling table, cantering with sharp white teeth. "I win every time!"

"What's your number?" calls out Mr. Tong, the fatso, joining him at the bar.

"Six, six, six!"

"That's fantastic!"

The chilled-out crowd at the table often cheers, and the opulent-faced matrons wave their ostrich-colored fans, cooing at him. Mr. Yu bows to the crowd and looks for another taker, only to see everyone looking cowardly.

"Anyone? Anyone?" he then asks with an obnoxious snarl.

All of a sudden, amid hushed voices, the doors open, and Ming walks in, looking shy and albeit strange. He walks up to the table and puts down his dollar bills and rolls up his white puff sleeves and says, "Give me wacko!"

As the lucky dice rolls, the phalanx of bingo numbers show again with bright solid colors, flashing, "six!" to the extreme.

"Ming, the lucky winner!"

The crowd then cheers, and Ming takes a drink and begins to breathe easier. Surely this was easier than doing all those pit diagrams in his notebook. And why so noble? He laughs admittedly, his tousle of hair flopping about like a shiny doppelganger.

As he keeps on flipping his cards and playing two dice, the sinister chard smoke of the room covers his face, and he takes on a sentimental look, his subway glasses fogging up with a cloud of morbid, ceaseless anxiety. He is suddenly a madman hooked on bosho, and the crowd again cheers him on, watching him win and lose some until his pocket is covered with solid gold bills.

"Why not every night, Ming?" coos some lady in a pink vest who eyes him with careful disdain.

"Ming is a wonderful scholar but also a man of true fortune, a man of the stars," says Mr. Fu, the proprietor of the palace, who giggles with a surly tongue and walks about, sticking fresh flowers in everyone's lapels. "How's that lovely wife of yours? Are you getting any respect?"

"I don't know, Mr. Fu. Life is tough."

"Then come here to get away from it all anytime! That's what it's for!"

"That's true, that's true!"

As the comical notes of some jazz music blare inside the room, Ming tries the slot machines and cackles and thinks with some hypnotic voice that all his life he has been searching for that magical number, the digits that will make him goddamn wild in the face—why try too hard? Why not just pull the mystical lever as they say in Venice?

As he thinks of the mysterious shaman, his heart shudders, and he puts another round coin in, crying a bit and thinking cynically of his so-called studies. Why try to be a gentleman and a scholar when life was so impenetrably dark? He was penning so beautifully when his world crashed, and now this, some preachiness! More nickels, more nickels!

***

Damp, secluded streets where the moon is sprite gold, a dream well of interpretive colors in a whorl. The infused layers of Harley smoke and the temple of propinquity where the thick dirt grows dried up with a thud. The end of the turnpike where the nation blooms with ardor, like some village of kind, rosy-faced children where aphrodisiacs are used like bones in a foul pot, the range of chicken feed like webbed stripes of stuffing—these too are found along the city's kitchens where the laundry hangs dry like white ghostly shirts in search of a name. Who's to say what's decent in these encampments of strange honor where obloquy and insult know no boundaries and stones are hurled like furlough on display and braids swing back and forth with no discourse? If you ply your path along the cobblestone roads, for fear of mean-faced congers and brickbats, fearing chicken blood along the path, crossing yourself, doing doublespeak at the light sign, you'll see the truth.

"Why so fearful?" asks the shaman who sees me shaking and holds my hand as I cross, his eyes full of deep, welled-up concern.

"It's nothing. It's just this inveterate depression," I say, my head clouded by thoughts of the coming afterlife on the horizon. The misfit dragons in the wind do their double turn, and the ice cream truck trundles forth with a tinkle of a singular bell that makes the children run forward in the thick fog where the swinging vines cross one another blithely and the wind crosses on the dragon terrace, knocking over the stone porcelains.

"It's the pseudonym for the city, the big Monkey Villa!" exclaims the one-eared monk with deep despair in his eyes, his casket of beers glimmering like glassy bowling pins in a bucket. How lofty his exultations, and how obsequious his manners. How he beats his brass gong and prays for Ming.

"He'll go to his wife as sure as the falling rain!" he exclaims with outstretched hands, his wide nostrils flaring out. As the mystic temple glowers in the background, I sigh and run toward Jackson Street past the whole nest of calligraphy and the wagging tails of the puppies on the sidewalks. All around is the rain making me drenched with the vicious downpour of the season.

"What can we say of these outrageous lives which are dangling in the mix?" says the shaman with a derring-do, moving after me in the warm, fluctuating rain with an upturned floral umbrella. "One day, it's the yin, and the next day, it's the yang—a sorry ensemble to say the least!"

"I'm not sure, Master Shaman! What can we say of the future of the city?"

"It belongs to these humblings. These dim sum eaters. These wild fortune-tellers. What else can I say?"

"What's the secret to retaining sanity in the snake pit?"

"It's to wear your rosy spectacles from heaven."

"Where are you headed?"

"To the Hotel L'Orange, of course!"

With a wink and a nod, he sails away in the midst. "I've got the Monkey-town blues but to beware of that deep blue funk which is too heavy for words, 'Why so dark?'" he says, laughing. "We only live once. What did you think of the gypsy? And Mr. Yee? And this whole imbroglio of matters?"

"I'm not sure. It surely is quite mythical."

"Then go in peace and eat your dim sum. And pet the little parakeet in the cage."

"What's the secret?"

"It's to do good and be good. That's lesson one."

"Gotcha."

"And stop kvetching about the rain!"

"I'm outta here!"

"And breathe the air of the common people like you know how."

As the lotus-colored umbrellas break up heavy in the downpour, the shaman then disappears into the night, and I'm left alone in the city to make heads and tails of the sinister fabric of the den of snakes, lofty as the temple as it scares me. With fascination, I hear the clop-clop of the shoes of the passing pedestrians and look at the wizardly faces in the mist.

I head to Yeo's to sup on turtle soup and give my three cents to the old men with their ragtime vanity and thrice-bred faces.

***

As the incoming jet storm enveloped the city in a savvy wet rain, the pink roses on Battery Street exploded into a fragrant bloom. Ming stomped home with an empty pocket and a silly smile on his face, his experiment of gambling coming to a final bust in the middle of the night. How the slot machines had misled him and the hot perfume of the stinking room had made him insensibly sickened! How the acacia hyacinth trees now mocked him as he walked this way and that, willy-nilly, taking his time in the fresh open air, his savings from the year gone in a quick shining flash!

"If it isn't Ming!" exclaimed Mrs. Wong, who had just come back to sup from Yeo's and looked at him with derision, clicking her heels. "Where could you be coming back from at this time of night? Don't you know the shaman is looking for you everywhere?"

"Oh, it's doomsday! Why don't you leave me alone, you old bitty? I've enough problems on my mind!"

"That wife of yours is sure to run off and leave you someday. Don't you know you're a mockery of the city?"

"Oh, bum off, Mrs. Wong. Why don't you head to the soda machine and have a Coke in the brain? You're all puff and smoke!"

"That's fine, Ming. I warned you—the whole city is talking about you!" And with a huff, she waltzed off in the other direction, her face looking like unholy fire, her dress a bright sapphire blue. It was as if she disappeared in a cloud of fine smoke, stuttering some keen nonsense about the city's unpredictable future.

Ming shuddered inwardly and kept walking until he reached home, a two-story brick which he and Alicia had bought up with Old Lady Wing's gimbo money. As he opened the front door, he walked in, sighing, his whole body in the power of a frenzied stupor. The house seemed empty, except for some old furniture and a few cobwebs stubbed in the corner.

"What's that? You're back?"

"My dearest Alicia—I'm home!" he called out drearily with a sigh.

"Where have you been?"

With a bit of starry blush on her face, her hair covered by tendrils of alarum, Alicia ran out of the kitchen to see him, her entire sentient being covered with suds-up tears. "How could you?" she exclaimed heartily with a sigh. "You've been gone for—the last two weeks!"

"It's nothing," said Ming nervously. "My drawings weren't going well, and I—"

"Where have you been?"

"Nowhere. Just out, hanging around."

"Do you have the money I gave you?"

"Why do you ask?" Ming replied, looking scared, out of sorts.

"You'll never guess what happened!"

"I'm pregnant!"

"Pregnant?"

"That's right!"

Ming laughed out loudly and put down his book of fancy drawings and felt lousy, as he always did when he did that. Despite all the crazy gambling he'd done, he was rewarded with this shock now, to be sure. He'd never been a father before, and now here was this surprising news. Perhaps he should have bought a better gift for her, the one he loved. Or a rattle at least! Surely, this was wonderful news!

"I was out gambling and lost all the cash!" He grinned sheepishly.

"Never mind about that—we're going to have a baby!"

"Do you mind being married to a poor scholar like me?"

"No, Ming. Why so insecure? And gambling like that!"

As the two romantics linked eyes, the plentiful acacia trees of the dusty orange field bloomed out in the dirt backyard, and the ancient *pipa* music played loudly, sounding boisterously. The terrace empty, the phoenix-colored chairs covered with enigmatic dust, the two danced to the fabled jazz music in the background, kissing softly.

"So you really don't mind me blowing all that cash in the casino?" he laughed wildly, his hot eyes on fire like a demon.

"Of course not!" she said, winking. "What do you think of Mrs. Wong? Isn't she a gas?"

"What do think of this name—Daniel—for the baby, if it's a boy, that is?"

"*Dan,* I like the sound of that."

As the heavenly gypsy music blared, their still passion exploded into wild flashes of light, and the night wore on. Outside, the sensuous rain poured upon the town, much to the surprise of the denizens. It was that simple flair of keen weather that made the people flock together in the keenness of opulent nighttime, chanting the name of dragons and phoenixes, purling gold.

As the old jade temple knelled its bell, ghosts chased their fortunes in the moonshine, making the yew tree leaves creak in the mud, leaving the aged imprint of posterity for those to ponder the coming days. The blue moon glistened like a clinking fairy-tale coin, bright as the palm of Buddha, so simple for the world to see.

PART III

THE FLOATING HEM

Like spiritual beatniks in search of a higher power, the hippies and the glam chicks on Jackson Street pray to the Buddhas in the store window, chanting *om* for better luck tomorrow. There are starry looks in their eyes, a hint of sarcasm on their lips, some clicking of the ruby heels. All about is the muggy temperament of past movie stars, of desperadoes, and of ancient rice matrons of the porridge pot with risible icons of dragon glory in the sky. Always incense-heavy, the righteous people of Chinatown move to and fro in the rain-flirt wind, their coal debris glistening with fulsome color, some faux pas of spring in their troubled eyes.

Off the cuff, I will wait here by the lucky sampan cat at the famous sushi shop on the corner, staring at the prismatic lights, peering at the tiny face of my watch, and dreaming of some lovely opium pipe with which to dispel my deeper heartfelt worries inside. As the loud traffic blares, the preeminent struggles of the cooler crowd become apparent: some *clickety-clack* of the older goose-faced women who scare, some pinochet ladies in rouge lipstick mouthing rosary, and some jade-faced ogres that move at a fast pinch with beckoning, faithful stride. All about some quick spill of evil congou in the electric bin air, some porridge-eating factory which will make the conch monsters leap forward, some balloon hoax of a life in which many rowdy people will spill the beans at once when the collective rays of the sun will shine on those choleric eyes of the glum. There's a bit of a hokum in the tarry streets, some shiny bijoux of flooded color that makes everything look like a barfly, upside-down cake, some afterthought of fall-out frenzy.

Like sudsy apple-faced children that chew their jooky sticks look terribly sallow in the motes of dust, the many clever denizens move in the absolute thrum of Polk Street and complain that they're just too superstitious, like their cunning forebears, that they actually believe in the ogre taglines of their fortune cookies, dreaming of the realization of the augury with each delicious crunch. "Confucius says do better," says one dreamy-eyed believer, rolling up her cut sleeves, some gimlet stars on her hard-worn spectacles. Her to-do hair is perm-heavy, and her eyes pop out like flirty exclamation points. She is on cue, living in a fantasy of rice, chopsticks, and burnt chop suey, a testament to the madness of the outrageous Chinese. Single eyelids close in indelibly in the sleepy afternoon, wisps of the sad, contagious moment. So much for the mah-jongg game she was about to play with her crony of six friends or those fried sensational sesame balls she was about to eat on a fantastic spur. She moves forward, off-kilter, on frittered toes, scouring the future skyline for some hint of the chosen hour and dances off in waves of fall-out memory, unable to come to herself under the bended cassia trees.

Under the opulent sun, the women appear to have six fingers on each hand, clinging to lavender fabric of the sea, stringy, dull-faced women of the dynastic accord of past times. They move with ticktock fantasy limbs, chiming in at inopportune moments, speaking of the secret passwords of the city, as if their appendages were made of solid rapier gold. These Chinese men have watches that melt into their stitched pockets, their staunch smiles like surreal fixes of indemnity. What lounge ideas they patch up in their ornery brains! What consummate lingo they have! I see them in the disturbed white fog, laughing like shamans and witches, an imbroglio of shame-faced monsters crouching about on second terms, flinging their copper rings and ties in the air like culled-out demons to the fore.

With pearly teeth and fob noses, the many women who call themselves witches walk about on clogs and pray to dragons-a-darkle and call out the naturalistic names of their ancestral grief. Who knows what unearthly life there is in their comedic eyes and their curly Q-smiles? They seem a saintly bunch wearing frippery and grim lace from the basement of their dusty-shaped houses, their feather mops covered with muddy stain-colored dirt. There is some quasi-sentimentality in their angelic touch, some leftover dreams of tomorrow at best. Why Monkey-town is like that: full of high jinks and two-touch gizzards and throaty, hot-scotch porridge. Some vanity of the extraneous muses in the frozen air.

"I get that painful itch to drive there every so often—so solve the parable of my so-called life," confesses one woman, a tourist at Sammy's who looks closely at the parakeet-colored headdresses at the miniature playing card and the viridian crickets which are lined up on the glass stand. She is in love with the odds and ends of Monkey-town, the utter *mismatch* of it all, the topsy-turvy houses, and the ping-pong effect of life. "I came here to see how truly colorful all of it could be. How strange people could be," she gushes out loud with a horrible gist.

Among the glossy alligator bags and the dimpled minks which glimmer in the scattered fragrant light, there are those sassafras-tinted dresses which are imported from Saigon, still skipping fresh in the plastic bag. Also lounging on the desk are the stationary frogs with squarish gold coins in their octo mouths, ready to leap out at you like diamonds. The underground world of Sammy's is rife with fun-loving ambiguity and deep contempt for the quotidian, you see. The sepia-colored kneesocks of the dolls which sit in the window make you giggle like a young child, and the manic-eyed old stuffed Confucian scholars, figurines from the Ming Dynasty era, are the stuff of archaic aping pleasure.

"Why that, Master Fong, is the heart of imagination and true ambition!" Mr. Yee calls out to him joyously as he walks about the store with his laces undone, his glass spectacles drenched with cymbeline hush-hush tears.

The furry leopards glower patiently from their dusty bowers, and Mr. Fong fingers their thin whiskers and hurries about quickly with a sashay blomtie. What misfortune there is in his bounty eyes, and what funny invectives he hurls at the winds to the fore? Like a truly animated figure with svelte feet, he rubs the Buddha's belly and looks after his nativity like a foolish bandit, rolling his eyes in the thought of some distant Shangri-la awakening.

As he walks about, his lolling pupils finally rest on a teakwood carving of a sleek-faced fisherman with an autumn leaf-shaped beard curved just so. The fisherman was holding one pole held by a string. "So lofty and yet so tiny—like the flaming eyeball of the Tao!" he exclaims thunderously, his wrinkled socks falling to his knees.

"It's from Beijing," says Mr. Yee proudly with a shrug of disbelief. "Why don't you buy it and put it on your mantel? It's a real decade piece."

"You've sold me," Mr. Fong says, searching for his greedy wad of bills. "I'm actually a creature of sentimental worth. Nothing moves me, except these sordid creatures of the East."

"Why sordid?" asks Mr. Yee. "Why not mystical? These carvings were bred from mist and light!"

"Whatever you say, Oswald. But put it in a bag and make it double snappy!"

"I see you have some place to go!"

"Back home to where the sampan sailors go!"

"That'll be two whistles and a peach for you!"

"And two demons and a snake, my friend!"

"Sold to the elegant Mr. Fong, zappo!"

***

On Geary Street where the golden zigzag bricks smell like hot sampan curries and the bilbo noses of children move amid squalor and fresh chutney, Mr. Fong sits in his entire study, admiring his many artistic pieces—the enchanting hexagonal mirrors, a dour Guanyin statuette, all murmuring in his secret shadow. How memorable his button-down cap and his white tooth squirrelly smile, his triumphant sidestep, and his elegant goatee, all remnants of an old Cathay that squirts directly from a shapely bottle of Kikkoman soy sauce on the dusty high-clef mantle.

"I can begin to believe what the old ancients did—and dance the dance of joy!" he exulted, thinking upon the miracle of acacia silkworms and the *terra incognita* of the planet, the oily thumbed pages of his *Analects* reader covered with tea stains. The dog-eared book, covered with cheap annotations and scribbles, served as an endearing testament to madness, to his curt speech. He ranted all day like a scribe, saying that things were part and parcel of his whole life, of the many foul demons that haunted him like bloated underground spirits, ghouls of the past reflective hour.

"Why try so hard to understand the entire universe when the motes of the world are under your red thumb?" he said, cackling blithely. There was a morose expression on his face that was grotesque, as if the beautiful gash on his forehead had become more damnable.

That oolong tea was served stoutly bitter in his cupped breath, some bit of a mental sop to his painful endeavors, those he likened to chosen experiments in extemporaneous posturing, which he confessed were no more than two feathers in the wind. His hair was like a cloud of passions, and his uppity nose bled when he read his romantic couplets too much on the side with a concupiscence. His leathery shoes exuded some anachronistic wonder, with damp shimmer of copper buckles which changed color with remedy, easily in the light, and he wambled this way and that to the kitchen and wondered to himself about the many lives a rosy-eyed Confucian could lead without courting mishap and furtive danger.

"It could be that painfully simple—to be a winning scribe of the countless dozen! To be peacock perfect, to be accounted that way for by your fourteen steps to straight heaven!" he let out with humbug, thumbing his thin beard with blustery hands.

To put it simply, he fingered his bright counselor's robe with a chiseled finger and plucked the lynchpin from his simper buttons and imagined he was a satyr on the go. He chortled with merriment to no end, as in lasting retribution, singing like a young sprite on cloud nine with an abacus in each hand. "A scribe of the times!" he confessed warily, smiling in his starry misfit gown which hung to his knees and was covered up with beige abracadabra sweat.

As he walked about the room toward the blooming tulips, he hummed a song of the ancients and pretended he was a saint of yore, of old times. The perfume of solitary incense in the room made him gag uncontrollably, and he felt nauseous, devoid of any open human emotion. *Why try so hard to imitate the greats when you were only so small-fry and so tiny,* he thought suddenly, full of spic. His was a twisted bonsai tree, which he had looked after for so many years with a calm devotion, suddenly appearing spiky and unruly in a most unbecoming way, so to speak, and haunting him with its fractious leaves. How duly out of kink everything seemed to be! It left him sore, with sinister belief.

To think it, that I am nothing but an old man with fading intemperate powers! he thought sadly, obvious with a doleful tear in his eye. Suddenly, his cow horn calligraphy meant nothing at all to him; and as he dreamt of the lovely parakeet at Yeo's, he could see it mocking him, saying that he was no more than an exalted pauper of the fading era.

With his slanted squid eyes milking tears of pain into his goose-down pillow, he crunched into his bed and lapsed into a storm of cunning depression. Surely, there was something he could do to absolve himself of this obsolescence! As he prayed to the holy gods above, he felt some shock effect in his heart, humbled himself on the incense settee, dreaming of sere clouds. Why should the beat go on and on? Perhaps tomorrow, a new kingdom would be found.

He chuckled then, looking at his face in the mirror, dreaming of Flora's beautiful fingers, and didn't care so much for his high-minded precepts after all. Only the gods knew how precious time was and how an old man with five whistles could conquer the entire world.

****

The new era was dawning on Chinatown on Battery Street where the hyacinth trees were blooming with fresh oranges. People in smashed-up vehicles were rounding about the slow lane, beating up pitter-patter traffic with smashed-up mirrors of disapproval. There were loud jaybirds crashing behind in the land of few and plenty. All over the city, in the fringe of hodgepodge cement, the Chinese wore their flashy gewgaws and made faces like holistic jack-o'-lanterns in search of a better, more conquistador name. High and low and up and down on Franklin Street, they were their best suits and warmest fox furs with hopes to see the season through just right. Just like those festive lunar boat people who had come before them fifty years ago, these were their blessed children with tousled, greased-up locks who had slant centipede eyes and wore wide platform shoes, spoke

chop-chop *Chinglish,* and spent their crumpled dollar bills in the madcap
burger shops complaining they wanted more and more.

With their distinctive gift for power linguistics, they had their
wispy pomade and flinty rings, their gemstones on their sandaled feet
symbolizing some dysfunctional bravura with the world, also some salvo
with their salty ideas of time. Snakelike and full of fiery conniptions,
they brought with them their frank nobility and their largesse of charms,
their abundance of haw flakes and lizardlike tails whopping in the milky
air. Theirs were the surreal numbers of ticktock watch and the manned
rocket of the moon station, the altruistic smiles of ingratiating grannies
with electric keezer blue hair.

Also present were the n'er-do-well charms of the gangster children
with their primitive *om* signs on their arms to hide their penultimate hurt
and hid their rakish fear from the loathing world. On summery days, out
in the fecund soil, they would practice tic-tac-toe by the Washington
Park playground, gunning down invisible enemies, leaving pennies in the
plastic piggy bank on the bench. As they squirmed about, they sneered at
the old men in gabardine who were playing chess in the park and belched,
stole their chess pieces, choosing to live life passionately with venom.
Under the longevity clouds, they played steal the bacon like squeamish
chickens and made the order of the day to belittle the gods and deacons
of wonderland. How fabulous their chop-chop words! How seedy their
glances!

"You think I like dim sum, but I don't like that shit!" screamed
Maybelle, one of four-year-old children who was wearing a sweet flounce
in her hair and preferred ice cream cones to most anything else. She
walked about the playground splashing Diet Coke in the wavy hair of the
other children and jangled her toy bracelets with soul power to summon
up the nectarines. Her jet braids fell forward on her shoulders like some
string of mighty sausages tightly pulled at the subterranean twixt, and
she spoke Cantonese, albeit poorly, cursing at the hanging Peking ducks
in the front store window, which glowered in the eyes.

"How ugly they are—with wings like that and tongues like that.
How hideous!" she awed to herself, playing with shiny marbles in her
dress pocket. They were a creamy whorl of dozen tossed out on the
dirt unceremoniously with a sprocket of fantastical glimmer. Maybelle

dreamt of deeper outer space and its host of reddish rings, its shimmer of cool sheen mist. What she would do now was come to her finer senses about it all, this robotic set of beings that lived in Monkey-town, about the men that teased her with their curtsy beetle-shaped eyes. She loved that, being in the center of things, but only if it meant that she got that, some egregious riddle that she could go away with.

****

With waxy-colored taupe fingers affixing postage stamps to the moon on six-by-eight postcards, Mrs. Wong dreamt of that serious cosmic touch of the afterlife and wrote missives to everyone she knew: her sisters, her mother, her cousins, her friends. She liked the inky resolve of the afterthoughts of the life she led and liked to put in plain letters to see the ersatz alphabet emerge on paper like a little stiletto of erstwhile dreams. *How keen!* she thought to herself as she braided her words together in fancy tropes and communicated her thoughts like a bandit of passing time. How tipsy her imaginary, segue words! She described Monkey-town and its host of fancy angels with deliberate care and pint of worry. Getting to the root of the problem, seeing its host of ruddy brown faces in the dust, she scribbled nonsensical ideas that made her titter off-key.

With her expensive eel-studded shoes and her shiny eyelashes, she was a paint pot of despair, all flash and no substance, like a briar ghost shimmering in capper threads. The precious seams of her dress were like thread escaping from a loom, and her eyes blinked vivaciously everywhere she went. *How's that for Mars red?* she thought, putting on her eye shadow. She liked to be garish to extremely voluble, cried when she thought of her postcards being read but never returned. How enviable the other people were on other planets, dabbling in their gobbledygook in their special trains of thought, as if they had ESP.

Tonight, she would turn the fire down real slow, stare into the starry pit of the bubbling congee pot, and see her watery ashen face stare back at her with a deep, unremitting growl. It was not knowing what was going to happen next that scared her. To be caught dead at Yeo's hankering for a special orange duck was not for the grace of her the best of the best— she'd rather sit here alone than be seen with those *bot pors* and Cantonese vampires who were mouthing off all their obscene epithets. *Why so lousy?* she thought to herself, her sweat coming up to her armpits, the mosquitoes in her nostrils, and her eyes flickering like leftover rice. The Cantonese have a way of making you feel bad in swarms, like penitent spider lovers or hot ants in the pants. What chance did she have of having a good time at Yeo's with all those matrons of deceit flinging wontons in her face and boasting of their inglorious lives?

Perhaps she'd fight the good fight and show up in a neon lime green feather boa and sing high opera in a choleric bash of the dozens. Why not make a fool of yourself dip into the pale mustard sauce with ghoulish frimpy fingers and steal the bok choy bouquet? It was all so ludicrous as it was! She wouldn't know a soul there, save the absurd Mr. Fong who was always there tipping his fedora to the minions! With the fat-faced maitre d' serving bingo punch, there would surely be wild stories to tell!

The entire day waned, and she sat in her musty living room crocheting exotic doilies, thinking madly about the people at Yeo's, wondering what would befall her if she didn't go. Like a little heady ant with sparse dreams, she watched the kettle pouf boil and tapped her bloodred shoes and said she didn't care.

***

Outsight, out of kink, the furled city like a picture parfait sinks like a meteor over the foggy damp sewers, over lefty feet and staccato-like breath, while pigeon-hearted men with long white hair walk the stiff beat in a fit of apoplexy, straining to hear the bass viola music from the upper glass windows in full ratso heat. It's not the glissandos that they love, but the sterling pizzicatos they adore, so flagrant as to be upper beat, some stretch of the salacious outré world where the buzzing bees add their muter color to the fresh batch of cloudy, fruity wares. The copper rosaries glimmering in the hoods on old witches are like beads of joy, and the itsy-bitsy rattles carried by the children look comic in the fairy-tale afternoon. With phoenixlike eyes, how they simmer in the dusk, looking so similar to pictures of old dowagers and matrons of plenty, the picture of demagoguery and reamed pulse.

Seething with seeds of scattered magnolia, the many people laugh by the watermelon stand, picking their slim teeth with dark thumbs and thinking ironic thoughts with scatter-brained energy. Who's to say what will spring up tomorrow like a golden sprig of parsley between the earth, and what grandeur there will be in the aureole of Mars? What anxiety of parables there will be on the second floor of Betty's Beauty Parlor where the small women with the splashy moles rush about with posh hairdos and clunky heels and heavy breasts?

I remember it all, the mad rush to the odd bars, the noodles, long and furtive in the flash pans beguiling me at every hour, the Monkey-town beat. What could make a young woman like me in love with the city but that sampan friction, those footnotes to another angelic century? I like to think the soy sauce squirted out the can at Yeo's directly in my eye, like a squid maker. That the moon was a bit simple, a double orb of fantastic order.

Why that, Master Shaman calls Mrs. Wong with her mess of curls bouncing up in fresh order at the banana stand, her lilac-blue dress glimmering in the waves of dust. As she is rushing up the stairs to the beauty parlor, she passes scores of women, many of them ginger-colored and damp-nosed, all vying for a fresh look. "How's that? My hair such a mess!" she says with a raggedy yawn and rushes past the oval A-window and into the beauty store where the cosmetic pumps are infusing all sorts of deadly chemical operations. Pastel hair dryers and webby hairnets and haughty cloaks for styling all set up for a purpose of utter fascination and instant repulse.

"I'm here for a touch-up, nothing fancy," she says, winking at Old Mrs. Lang, the head hairdresser sitting in the corner with the stinky baby perfume, the donut-ringed eye shadow, and the super-pouty lips. "Can you do it just as you did it before—real spring curls with a hint of sixties finish?"

"Sure thing, Mrs. Wong. You are our best customer! Why don't you take a seat?"

With a breathy laugh that morphs, she takes a seat, and they put an apron around her neck, and she stares at the long mirror where her wavy-navy face appears like a severe Modigliani in full tilt. As she takes in the years, she sighs and dreams of her former fragile face, which was all pink skin, and flighty goose eyes, rainbow cheeks, and perfectionistic dreams. As she drums her tip-tap fingers on the lacquer tiles, she remembers the dark secrets she has kept in her coven heart, the various people she has loved, and the horrible mistakes she has made. She think it is a deepest miracle that she keeps coming back to get these curls, the way a car gets its fuel.

"You know you spend so much on these curly pins!" says Martha, the beautiful assistant with the greasy tub of curlers standing in back of her. "Why do you come so often?"

"I have nowhere else to go, Martha. Chinatown is just four streets wide. It's a no-man's town!"

"Why don't you hang out with your children?"

"I don't have any—all I have are climbing plants that climb up to the sky, terrible I think."

"And why not children?"

"Too expensive—I could never afford to bring them up. Besides, I just don't have the time."

"How is Mr. Wong?"

"Boozing and gambling as usual. What else can I say? The man's a mousetrap!"

"What kind of alcohol does he like? He sounds cute."

"XOXO. What else would he drink?"

"That's *expensive stuff!*"

"He's a real operations wizard. Doesn't come home until the late hours! Don't ask me anymore questions!"

With an itinerant growl, Martha finishes up her damper curls, and they move her square to the blow-dryer where she sits underneath the big fishbowl heat glass and reads her glossy magazines. She's done it a thousand times—read her magazines, drank her tea, and had her suburban dreams finagled there like fresh finger cotton candy.

It's the big splash bingo! she thinks to herself, lulling herself into a lazy hip sway, dreaming of African dance music and neon cars and flipping the page to each loony advertisement in the magazine, thinking of all the ace people in the city, the wild destinies of others. Why in Chinatown? Everything seemed caught up in an abstruse teabag for abuse but exploded once you left its dangerous perimeters and became a sweet foolish confetti. Why not leave Chinatown forever? She could always move to one of the suburbs in San Francisco, or elsewhere, to be sure, but she liked this famous tenement of words and its cache as poor as it was. She liked living in the *fragmenta* of a live museum to be in the arms of a crazy hotel. She didn't mind being the matron of the dark frail skeleton, the screaming gorgon tiger.

"You seem to be in deep thought, Auntie Wong," said Sibyl, another one of the assistants who noticed her drifting off. "What on earth could you be thinking of?"

"Nothing," she snapped. "Just dreaming of the usual-usual."

"What are cooking for dinner tonight, dearie?"

"Nothing special—fish congee and snow peas with shrimp, I think!"

"I hear you're a wonderful cook, Auntie Wong."

"That's all hearsay, just gossip, my dear."

"You're too modest, Mrs. Wong."

"Not at all, Sibyl. Why don't I pay you the amount?"

As she saunters to the desk and pays her mean wad of green lettuce bills, she grimaces and looks in the mirror at her famous curls and thanks Mrs. Lang, the owner, with the riffed opaline glasses and the punk leather shoes. "Why, that's the best hairdo I've ever had!" she exclaims, laughing out loud like the plain druthers.

"You say that every time!"

And with a twinkle of the magical wind chime, she rushes out the door with her alligator purse and her curls bouncing up and down. *To the bakery,* she thinks with a soft, elegant trace of glitter on her tweaked eyebrow. Why, this was mission of the Chinatown savior in the throes of phlegmatic sorrow on the rise.

***

At the Paradise Bakery, she sits and waits, the sliver of a woman eating her red-bean pastries with a brown thumb and pelican skin. Old Mrs. Wong sits and bemoans her everyday mussed-up life and mourns the *sufi* world, mourns Chinatown with its flashy suburban eyes and its caustic drowned-out voices. *Why, that is the rhythm of the downtown crowd with heyday colors and dapper curse, its gumshoe charm,* she thinks.

Like a woman born of newborn tea leaves, goose feathers, and high temperament, she taps her shoe and finds her lava syllables of rice, fire, and water, chooses her athwart destiny. It's that oval, egg-shaped face of hers she sees in the fry glass window that mocks her, makes her think she's mummylike, a porcelain figure from another deceptive age of soft angles.

Busybody, laughing muse, unaccountable droll fix, she could be anyone's flibbertigibbet; she was giddy as those balloon-voiced children on Jackson Street she passed every day. Why had she been so mean to Alicia? She didn't really know. Some judgmental vice in her, something snapping like a quack bird with cruel morbid eyes.

She had made her terminal mistakes before, had surfaced like a giant blue wave when she hadn't wanted to, spoken too many words like a vicious *bo por* when she only should have been that diminutive like one, two, three. She had spoken so many words, riffed, confused sentences, and felt that tug of the ample heart warning her that she had said too much.

She hadn't meant to be that duly invasive, that loud, and that definitive in her touch. Too much to say about the beatific world when she couldn't even pluck feathers with one fretful hand, much less press pennies into her soft, aching palm. She felt so damned helpless inside, just like a frail Buddha with cupped hands glowering on a soft pillow that might be tipped over by the sentry wind.

She had seen her share of pickaninny, of wear and tear, of horror tragic shrieking by the shop windows of frittered time. She had seen those myriad creatures of the Chinese-American cloth go batty in the night living in Chinatown proper trying to find lost taboos and hidden talents for love and passion. All that simple rice porridge could make an old woman go crazy with hurtful talons in the night! And the way the wind blew off the salutary hats of all the people, leaving them stark naked, the sheer nonsense pouring out of the catfish mouths of the children who were playing insensible tic-tac-toe! It was indefensible to say how the charms of Chinatown wore off in the lesser evenings like some sprinkle of magnolia perfume, tilting things about with their dreamish, coulicoue parameters.

As she drank her dark coffee and put a little pinched center in the top of her pastry with her pewter fork, she thought of Mr. Wong and his watermelon moustache, of his incessant boozing, and sighed out loud. What made life bearable in Chinatown was these parched moments of time, the twinkling bells of ardor in Mr. Lim's toy store that bespoke the charms of the patient hours and the stereotypical monomaniac whispering voices in the backdrop of the temple on Polk Street and the adorable T-shaped hats the young children wore on the playground at Washington Park while writhing in the white dust for some sanity and the wonderful lectures of the shaman!

As she crossed her legs, she thought of all the enlightened people she had met during her years in Chinatown and laughed, remembering how quickly the years had flown by. It was a life born of pertinent false cues, baby bok choy heads on fire, and a variety of lustful dragons, a hybrid of dreams imported from the realm of the Far East. Of pretty-faced demimondes, revenants, and a crop of silvery ghetto speakers in the hotcha blend of hours. It was that easy to find a revelation of oneself in these silvery ace puddles on the street.

PART IV

FLORA'S WORLD

Flora Chew bloomed slowly like any other woman, in the throes of it, some nervous apoplexy chewing her apish nails in the nursery where she would stare closely at all the gerbera daisies with a vain, disinterested eye. With billowing sleeves and shimmering, opaque hose, she looked like the very insane picture of a female pirate, some antique relic which emanated some basement-heavy glamour glowing in the battalions of light.

A mousy, insouciant type, she lived on 212 Clay Street all her life and prayed with the gentle hands of the devout and the pious, receiving kvetcher's rain only intermittently throughout the frozen years. The basement in which she lived was a musty utopian underworld wracked with silvery wet cobwebs and extreme Barbie-like fauna, with the sturgy perfume of termagants and the wicked cherry light of ghosts of her previous life, which had flown by like a toss-feathered cuckoo bird. Chipped porcelain saucer-colored ocean stared her in the eye in the china closet and roseate water paint peeled off at the *quattro* edges bled with a ghastly off-color hue that made you gasp for breath.

It was that sheer insipid lamplight that flooded everything and everything in the room—the scratchy beige silk stockings, the spongy ruby lipsticks, the pouchy aprons, the U-shaped spatulas gemmed up with thick white translucent grease that made everything purely imagistic. Flora was that unaging Chinatown dolly you see preening in the black 'n' white flicks, an Anna May Wong archetype with the outlandish crooked hairdo and the flocking birdcage hat, the silkworm sweaters that sing fearlessly to you in the virulent break of springtime with a bit of luminosity. She also cooked a mean baked clam-spaghetti, made it hot and steaming with a layer of warm goat cheese that was gooey all the way to the top, the kind of food Chinese people long for after eating rice for the thousandth time.

"Stop that! Stop that awful trap of yours, Flora!" the neighbors would call out to her when she took out the trash in the mornings, letting her truculent, o-b voice sail higher into a straight soprano, imitating the Platters's song she had heard on her recorder. There was no instant party punch for her, a long way for her to become a professional vocal singer. In some ways, she broke glassy windows with her awful cacophonic voice but liked to hear it sail higher into the electric bonny air just the same for a painful moment. Wasn't that what it was about, waking up the sweeping euphoric world with a keen karaoke beam of super eclectic wonders?

Inside the tiny heart of her basement, she looked into her miniature vanity mirror, in which she never aged, looked sixteen years of age, and had straight edge-up bangs like some China doll with a glittery, besotted eye. She let the whorlish words rise out of her taciturn mouth and felt it *cold*, the dampened feelings she felt for Mr. Fong. Was it not ridiculous for a man to give her gerbera daisies and purple ones at that? She painted her long tendril-like nails a wild lavender with a tiny chute brush, chanting his name like a pained word for pure isolated loneliness.

Now she would sit upright on the bright, delicious meditation cushions, dreaming of only him and watching the chintz motes of scintillating dust fly in the basement where her many fine dresses were hanging helter-skelter in the rough closet, watching her like old frock friends from high times. Ribbons of keen hypnotic airs and round velour pieces she had picked up at consignment stores with fancy 1940s zippers that beguiled indeed; some odd French headdresses that cast a deep invisible spell on you when you stood in the right pompous intrusive light, a floating Spanish twill skirt that was all-about-me red and worn just once in the store with kipper élan. *That too had cost a pretty penny,* she thought to herself mournfully.

"Now tell me, Flora, if you are so rich, why do you bother spending your time in Chinatown with a man as strange as Mr. Fong?" the landlady had said to her the other day, smirking at her as she put on her set of expensive clothes. The thick double layers of lipstick she wore!

True. Mr. Fong was an archaic and was like an old Confucian scholar who wore laughable kneesocks that didn't match and had a garbled accent, but wasn't he an honorable man? Didn't he know all the annotations to the old pedantic books? Now Flora soused, dreaming of a more handsome type, but her heart melted in the very end. She felt passionate about these so-called pedantic nerds!

"Serves you right, Flora. You've spent your whole life in the basement trying on lipsticks of different various colors. Why don't you go out with Mr. Fong for a change?" the landlady came again with a snouty drivel.

Flora shuddered. She knew she was uniquely gifted and florid but oh-so-damned shy in that sylvan way that scared people off, and who knew what they were thinking when they met her when she only said two curt syllables of silliness and nothing more? She was on the brink of saying something pertinent each time, some equation of loftiness that would impress indelibly with a pointed cued-up delight. Lord knew how she tried when the man would leave her in a quick huff! Some heartbreak indeed had followed, until she met Mr. Fong, who was all jollity and sampan sandwiches and seemed to care more about her peacock green eye shadow than the fact that she had a speech disability. Shy; Lord knew she was shy!

She sighed sweetly and looked at the shiny hard wood floor, winking at the glitzy iridescent spider in the webbed corner and began to comb her rough hair with a rosewood comb and knocked her knees together with a careful disdain to be sure. True, she hadn't felt this great in years; it was as if there was a real kinky curl in her hair, as if her nails had grown two inches overnight! She didn't care if she were just fishing for seminary good luck out there in the whole universe again. Her sheer karma was changing again, like the impulsive color of her jade ring that had been given to her by her deceased grandma. She felt this surging in her breast that Mr. Fong was the *right one,* not just some inveterate ghost passing by in commonplace suitor threads. She liked to think that Chinatown was full of wonderful happenings, and here was one of them: a Confucian fobbie that she loved, courting her in high, elaborate style.

"What's that—that confused smile you have on your face? I haven't seen you look this great in years! To think that you painted your nails three times!" expressed the landlady, laughing heartily with her.

"That's true, that's true!" said Flora demurely, looking at her purple nails and blushing like a child.

Birdlike, she would cling to her troth and wear her jade rings to sleep tonight in the city, dreaming of Mr. Fong. She would name all the blooming flowers in the nursery after him and nod with wild, toothy mirth. Why, all her years in Chinatown had flown by with a summery bliss, and now this, some mystical magic to haunt her. As she stared outside the basement window, past the blinds, she thought, she could espy the moon, which covered everything in fragrant effusive light. The manifold figures of the city were moving about like vigilant toys or silhouettes of time; and off and away, the fog covered with the city like an off-the-shoulder mink.

****

With a few trickle of flurried notes, Emerald Palace was jazzed up to high electric voltage with a brass trombone and an electric bass; the whole room lit up like a frenzied zoo of lightning with pea sprouts dripping from everyone's laps like stolid paint. The stupor of the light drifted from the left window onto sweet Ms. Eliza's blushed cheeks and down onto her white gloves which lifted an ivory chopstick above her plate of half-chewed pollack.

She had been waiting three hours for Flora to show up and had just lost her patience, crushed her rose napkin in a ball, and tipped her chilled mai tai over when the door opened, and in walked a svelte figure in an orchid-beaded gown carrying a bunch of violets on fire. It was none other than Flora, looking comically ecstatic under a thick layer of makeup, *caked*, as it were. Her eyelashes were like clear mosquito wisps, and her lips pouted proudly like a goldfish. She didn't look her age.

"Didn't I tell you I'd show up?" she said excitedly, waving her hands back and forth as if she were doing some sago-sago. "Anything to please the crowd. And here's my saltshaker."

To her left, guffawing like the ringmaster of ceremonies, was old Mr. Fong in a top hat and silk tie, with jimmy spats to boot. His squishy eyes glistened with comic bedlam, and as he walked, he took the liberty of taking Flora's hand and kissing it passionately. His normally dusty appearance so caught up in the world of books and pedantic torture was now lit up by romance and the apercu of distinctive lovemaking. How apparently droopy his eyes were, now glowing like a wandering panther in the midst of it!

"I'll have you know that Flora speaks of nothing but you!" said Eliza to Mr. Fong, staring at him straight bull ring in the eye, with a bit of keen mischief. "I hear you are of the old Confucian stripe!"

"Books and nooks and following the Tao and all those *non sequiturs!*" he said nonchalantly. "I'm a straight man, not to mislead any woman's heart."

"How so, Mr. Fong? Are you a boozer? Someone who drinks like a fish, a whoremonger?"

"Pooh-pooh on that! I'm the spiciest of the spice. A nice scholar who never tosses the dice and brings home the catfish on time!"

"Just so, Mr. Fong, you have an objectionable color about you. I hope you are the sweetie you're pretending to be! Take a seat and have some boiled fish." Eliza clapped her hands and batted her lashes; it wasn't every day that you met such horly hors!

As Flora and Mr. Fong sit down at the table, the waiter came by with an order of swamp martinis and deep-fried wonton strips which *seethed*, and Mr. Fong shuffled the deck by smiling winningly and letting out a burp.

As the table turned its attention to him, he dug into his fish and rolled up his old sleeves and sat like a specimen of curiosity, putting his arm around Flora who looked a bit nervous.

"Mr. Fong is a Luddite of the first order that can tie your shoelaces, I presume!" says Eliza, laughing with a silly grin.

"And make good wontons, dear!"

"He memorized the *Analacts* from front to back and makes good octopus soup!"

"Stop laughing at me!" he said, blushing outright.

"His calligraphy is first-rate, and now he has a girlfriend," said the waiter, elbowing him with a one-two.

"Does he wear his socks in bed?"

"Stop joshing me!" said Mr. Fong with a mawkish, extraneous smile.

"How does he make love, with a dictionary?"

"He uses pin yin with his lips, and brushstrokes are off when he kisses."

As they lambaste him with affectionate put-downs, Eliza softens and says that Mr. Fong is the "best fobbie in Chinatown there ever was!" He can take it, the jibes and off-color remarks and the whole fountain of lily green daiquiris as long as he has his Flora. As the longish silk curtains redound some mote of light in the room, his squash-colored face expresses some keen satisfaction with the food and the company, and he laughs, guffawing like an elusive scion in high druthers. The whispery gossip about him spread from table to table, something about him leaving his Confucian studies to begin a more lucrative profession. Something about him not having enough cash to make it in the world of Chinese quackery. Some two-bit words about him leaving his poetry behind to pursue a life in the bookkeeping industry. It didn't bother him one bit.

****

At Ng's Shipping Company the next day, Mr. Low looks worried, piling in the frozen fish from the cargo truck and smoking his brown capered cigar, his frizzled hair a glowing mop of distraction. *Why, C-town is nothing but a distinction of drab countenances, of sour acquaintanceship, and of holy conundrums to the hilt,* he thinks to himself. He can't make heads or tails of the city's beat or path the way everyone rushes in at once and buys sturgy and sea bass on ancestral worship days, whether they are stripped for cash or not.

A rich man, Mr. Low sniffs at the common throng of C-town and dreams of more expensive things, but settles to please the people with his stuffed octopus and packaged whale jerky for snits and saints. What makes the shipping industry tick, he thinks, is the pitiful stomachs of the ethnic dozens who inhale the stuff on Tuesday, Thursday, and Saturdays with their congee and pride of Hong Kong bawdy customers who scream for their shark's fin soup with bawdy. What he needs is a good man to take over his bookkeeping duties.

A nice coolie who is keen on taking over half shift, a good old Charlie with a keen eye for the ledger, he thinks to himself, chuckling, smelling the unctuous stink of octopus blubber around him like the dickens. It wasn't two weeks before he took down the HELP WANTED sign down from his little window overhead and saw Mr. Fong's dark celebratory face nodding in agreement with his talks.

"Now you sit here and total up the daily sales in fish, whole goods, and octopus blubber, old chap. You can do that well, can't you?" Mr. Low said, choking on his bit cigar and staring at Mr. Fong's age-old glazed face with suspicion and disregard. Something in his drab albeit brilliant countenance bespoke centuries at the wheel, some real hornet power, some possibilities of other planets conjoining with the stars. Who knew what the old man could do if you paid him by the hour?

"I need someone with a steel-iron brain who can think fast, mop up the room, and keep the shipments going . . . make sure there's enough shark, octopus, and fish, variety of all kind for all the people coming in."

Laboring at the kitch like a secret genius, Mr. Fong saw winter nights in his heart upturned by wheezing and conniption fits by coughing fits and ague. How could he explain to Mr. Low his predilection for the *I Ching* and the ancient rites and the way the sages melted his heart when he read the *Tao Te Ching?* He was a true poet at heart but had no knack for solid bookkeeping to be sure. He had flunked arithmetic four times in grammar school, earning the teacher's respect for his beautiful round handwriting, and been made to wear a dunce cap that made him look oh so outrageously callow. To think it, now, that he would sit on a wooden stool at Ng's Shipping Company and watch the numbers on the ledger! The very idea of it made his heart turn over like an old sausage in a steel frying pan.

"Okay, Charlie, then stand up straight and stop looking at that picture of my wife!" said Mr. Low, rubbing his hands together, straightening his tie in the mirror, and looking at the clock which ticked with a vim. These old Confucian men were hard to come by, slow to speak and think, but sure to agree with you. *A good hire to be sure,* he thought! Who else who sit there like a turtle and do the numbers while he had a good time shooting pool?

"Now listen here, chap. I'm going out for a good three hours while you watch the store. If anyone comes in, just wave this fish jerky at them and do the books like I said. You're a *ding-hao* match for this job! And I'm out the door!"

As the clock struck two, Mr. Fong shuddered in his lanky give-a-way bones and let his teeth chitter in the cold frosty room filled with the stink of perverse-smelling fish and octopus pieces. He dreamt of his lovely Flora with her catty eyes and her sharp hips and imagined her laughing with him over a pile of whale blubber. Her sudsy mouth and her holiday teeth were all the inspiration he needed to get the job done. As he pulled the wooden stool over by the heater, he drew his sweater closer to himself and began to look closer at the books at the ledger where the many screaming red ouster lines denoted the everyday commissions. So complicated and confused it made it heart hurt. It was at that point that he heard the tinkling of the misty bell on the door and the loud laughter of an elderly banshee woman with a high-pitched shriek. He knocked over the inkstand and let out a loud high whoop! It was his first customer.

***

"Mr. Fong, what are *you* doing here?" said Mrs. Wong suspiciously who burst in suddenly through the doors to buy whale blubber for her daily cup of tea broth. She was dressed, from top to bottom, in dark black cloth, and her skin had a bright blue mole on it right next to her upper lip so as to resemble some rude punctuation of sorts. Her narrow eyes glimmered, like some wonderful bijoux, and the hat she was normally seen wearing about the garden she worked in was replaced by a jeweled toque that came square off her straight jet-lined hair. Her sunburned skin melted into her clothes, and she seemed all of one snide picture.

"Why aren't you at home lying in the bathtub with your Hong Kong prickly foot?" she cackled. "And reading your primers of saintly love from *Jing Ping Mei?*"

"I was just hired today, Mrs. Wong. And enough of your blather! You are making my nostrils flare up!"

"Doing it for Flora, I see . . .," she said in her very nosy, intrusive manner. She couldn't help but make offhand colorless remarks. It was her wont!

"How about it, Mrs. Wong—buying some whale blubber and sparing me your remarks? I'm a business man now—proper and proper!"

"You're nothing but an old bastard in rat's clothing! Lord knows at the next Chinatown annual supper, we'll make you hit the gong with your head!"

"That's your head, Mrs. Wong! And it's this thing to be respectful! Your astrology signs are not very propitious indeed!"

"Just give me the whale blubber, Joe!"

"Duo xie!"

As Mr. Fong let out two puffs of dark green smoke tendrils out of his cigarette and handed her some packages of whale blubber, he burped and put the numbers in his little leather ledger and looked nervous. He put a pep pill in his mouth and sucked for air and let out a loud belch and looked at the roaming eerie clock and prayed so no one would notice. Every day for the past year, he had prayed to the vile fire-breathing god of supernatural fortunes, hoping they would answer his deep plea for a lonely cause, and now here he was up and up covering up the spot on the ledger where he had cheated. Indeed, no one would notice!

As soon as Mrs. Wong left, he began to get bored, to daydream about his Flora, and to doze into fated propinquity, the thick locks of his gray hair curling up to one side like a big oceanic wave of comic lusts. As his stomach itched, he decided he might try some of that exotic whale jerky that was really expensive and ripped the pouch open and snarf it down with his rapier teeth, *achooing* all the while. All that tough jerky was making him dizzy, he thought, and as he let loose into a cozy nap, the drippy ink ran all over his shoes, and his seething pillow of hair fizzled with the stinky perfume of whale entrails, a dream so wonderful and potent that he slept fitfully until six o'clock.

***

"Ho loy!"

With a big thump and a heady rap of knuckles on his face, Mr. Fong awoke to see Mr. Low screaming, punch tomato red at him in the store, shocked to see him sleeping on the slow job surrounded by copious pints of opened whale jerky and a mocked-up ledger of sorts. With amorphous inky stains on his long silk white gown and jerky breath pouring out of his octo mouth, his bushy eyebrows went up and down, while Mr. Low jerked him from the wooden stool and yelled invectives at him, calling him *lousy* and *incapable* and *senile pudding*.

What was an old man with poignant kneesocks, incalculably mismatched at that, supposed to know? He was too busy reading *Jing Ping Mei* at home, copper tea stains on the same page each time at that, to care, or suppose a career in the whale-jerky business and couldn't do complicated bing numbers to save his life! He knew how to play the *pipa,* how to wax the left waxy corner of his moustache, and how to tie an invincible bowtie, but God knew these intricate figures of deceit were beyond him!

"As a proper Confucian, I reject your job and its requirements of worldliness!" Mr. Fong smirked with thin tapered lips as he got up off the floor and dusted the mendacious dirt off his aquiline nose. Besides, the whale jerky was giving him a herpeslike condition and didn't taste good anyways. Who said the great monks had to go out into the misty world to prove their utter saintliness? He would sit by his lofty ideograms in his little house and stir the scintillating blue ashes in his funny chowder pot and close the tiny door to the outer world! To hell with shameless Ng's!

"And to you, old man, the old one-two! Out the door! And stop eating all my whale jerky!"

Mr. Fong shrugged and put on his shapely green fedora and got his pewter cane and sauntered to the door with a salty tear in his eye. Truly, he had had his heart set like a meteor on higher investments in the world, like getting that fat paycheck and buying Flora dinner for starters. But what use were cosmopolitan endeavors when it meant bending and heaving and sticking your hairy nose in a ledger all day to see vicious numbers biting at you with a chimp? He was a freeman, a Confucian, a scholar who was studying the practa of the stars with his brown thumb. With a sudden twitch of his fingers, he could make lightning appear and disappear in the whole sky and, with some cinched religiosity, make the hot water run into his bathtub so he could contemplate Zen while tickling his Asiatic tummy. True, he was out of work; he was nothing but a Buddha on the streets.

***

A story of congers and congou. Like a silver sampan whistle that has blown for too long or some pellucid crab fingers that have been dipped too heavy in pearly ice-up cream, Mrs. Wong can't keep her cool any longer, stomps on the wilted mildew fern in her frosty lawn with a snip, and decides the world's not worth thinking about. *Why that,* she thinks to herself glumly, thinking of all veritable brouhahas in the making at large, the clammy octopus soup she was boiling for herself that went sour at the last moment. How was it that people were always getting together in ill-famed Monkey-town for these lovely round-about fetes and breaking apart like the clatter of butter and cheese in a spiritual blender filled with vast cosmic ingredients that she couldn't afford? She was all that, riffed, elegant, and childish wonder one day and palpable blather the next! There was no telling which anonymous cosmic dark door she was going to walk through next! Only the mystical shaman knew!

In the big-telling city, the vamp estate winds blew securely through each dim sum hut and disturbed the wizened old citizens of this lightning fast town into a ruckus of sure beset charms. How their stiff beatific hair stood on end and how ghastly tan they looked in their V-necked Hawaiian floral shirts, playing banjo ditty for the last time! It's that erstwhile smugness, that rogue sensibility in their flirtatious eyelashes that will do them in, make them rogue figureheads of the last decade, make their scented rice bowls turn over upside down, notes Mrs. Wong, laughing in a Spanish dress as she passes by in a blur on Jackson Street, her lipstick smothered on thick juicy carmine lips. How their many children and their children's children all hailed the holy Buddha with the same curt call of absolute love, with that distinctive religiosity that made them go bitty blind in the night. How they clung to it, like some succor or saccharine sugar candy that made them go bingo with wildfire in their flashing faces. How the babies made mean talk of it in their sleep.

I sometimes think that if I had not come to Monkey-town, had not seen the rosy eccentric patterns of umbrageous shadows on my walls directing me in that strange course, I would have chosen something absurd to do anyway, like burn a thousand ghoulish dollars or buy a silly, expensive polka-dot chapeau for a circus clown. C-town, a vanity seer sucker of inner dreams, some vast milky struggle of the soul, could be that—my operative hideout—an dirty snake alley of mist and mints, of torrents and torques, of which I had never known. Those sour spidery spur windows of vacant light cracked in the gaseous middle, those cruel red Buddha eyes on the face of Mr. Lim charming the entire place until the damned poltergeists departed, and the elated phony accent of the old women's fingernail varnish of the hinder times we had remembered. It all beguiled to me, oddly colored grotesque, like the stupor of a frozen light.

In a supermarket on Geary Street, I decide that I will defy the gods and see the world at large from aisle to aisle, see the blue-colored frost along the mussels in a package melt superlatively like dapper rings in 3-D space, pick out the best ones for myself. I will be the choosy one, pushing my nosy fingers past the yellow boxy tempura packages and oohing and ahhing over the dried flaky banana strips, which sulk, taking my time looking at the kooky coconut heads, and seeing which ones will suit me best.

The old *frata* women who are terribly dried up in the face with the faded, fleshly cheeks will chide me for not buying the right gooey sauces, the just-so brands of x-brand cornstarch to make the puddings thick and delectable. *Chee-sing! Crazy!* They'll taunt me as I pick up my salty shrimp chips, my joy-colored soft drinks, and my deep-fried salacious string beans on the run. It's the bevy of Asian junk food I love, and I eat it by the ton, buying it every week, shocking the many people in the grocery store with my consummate beatnik centurion love.

"Jenna is a fast-food junkie and has a case of the Chinatown lovies!" says Mr. Song, the grocer, who totals up my packages and gives me a gross smirk. "Where's the bok choy and the shitake? How come you're not buying for your grandma?"

"I'm just passing into town, Mr. Song. I don't live here."

"That's good for you—there's nothing here but swirls of disgusting punch and fog. What brings you to this land of perfect O Chinatown?"

"The dim sum, it's always the dim sum."

"What else?"

"Anything that's super fun. I'm always looking for hot items and interesting variety stores."

"Have you tried Mrs. Sook's perfume store on Battery Street?"

"What's it like?"

"Cheap perfumes from Shanghai and around the world! It just opened. You gotta try it!"

"I'll take the tip. Thanks, Mr. Song!"

As I head out the door, he motions to me and whistles and says, "Don't forget to ask for Chrysanthemum Potion No. 35! It's a killer! My wife loves that shit!"

****

At Mrs. Sook's Apothecary on Battery Street, the sign twinkles bright red in quaint colors, and the golden arch doors look formidable, doubling up with grotesque, gothic handles. Mrs. Sook, a tiny arch hippolike woman in her late sixties, sits on a tiny wooden chair before the cash register, staring soothingly out the oval glass window, her long arch talons pinched with cheap colors. Her ripped hose is taupe black and scratchy, and in the muted background is the melisma of Cantonese opera that she warbles along with every refrain, making her that batty, her tiny round nose glittering like a sideways trophy.

Those eclectic perfume bottles, numbering in the pale hundreds, look like glassy miniature and see-through ships filled with precious seething liquids—ambergris, opaline, chrysanthemum, teakwood, and lilac to name a few on the list. Bawdy, balloonlike ship bottles that are blown up with gooselike pleasure and are filled with the pleasurable scent of hours, of deep lust for the inveterate dream that is known a sinner Cathay. Some scents to pass the hours with daffodil anxiety.

As I push open the door a miniature crack, the little store bell tinkles with an interpretive melody of hours, and Mrs. Sook sits up suddenly straight and looks at me with angry eyes, as if I'm to be that lost soul of the seven seas, an intruder to the fore. Startled, she brushes her fussed-up hair and throws down her crumpled Chinese newspaper and says something unintelligible rather smugly and laughs out loud in a secretive hiss.

"Why, you're Jane Wu's daughter! I can tell with the soft wispy eyes! And wearing all that makeup, how *special!* To think it, after all these years, I could recognize you. Your mother and I used to play tennis together. She's a wonderful woman."

"How could you tell? I mean I just walked in this store like a stranger. Why, that's *amazing!* You know my mother? Mrs. Sook, it's just so great to meet you."

"And you too! What's your name, doll?"

"Jenna, Jenna Wu."

"And what brings you to Chinatown and to my special little shop?"

"Mr. Song sent me, and I have this yen for collecting perfumes. It smells damn wonderful in here!"

"Well, he sent you to the right place—we have over a hundred perfumes here—what's your lotto?"

"I'm not sure—what do you recommend?"

"How about this little one over there—the Chrysanthemum No. 35?"

As she echoes the name of the nimbo perfume Mr. Song recommended, her salty eyes widen, and she looks at me a bit suspiciously, far too closely for my own comfort. As she sits back on her wooden chair, she bites into her starched plate of eco noodles and draws her crinkled paper close to her again, looking uncomfortable, with a mean stripe of pernicious giggle.

"It's an adventurous miracle perfume—they found it in the tomb of the Dowager Tze Shi who was holding the valve-shaped exotic-scented bottle next to her heart when she was buried long ago with the other puppies. It was the only way she could make the great emperor love her at all times! What do you think? Do you want to buy it—there are some powerful aphrodisiacs in this vial!" As she puts the quoted perfume in my shopping bag, she smirks and looks a tad unkindly and laughs out loud again as if caught in a private joke.

"It's a must-have! I'll take it!"

"Put it on your dresser-drawer, and I assure you you'll have dreams of bosh."

"I look forward to it—and how can I thank you?"

"Just say hello to your mother for me, and keep coming back!"

As I run out the door, the sting spray of lilac and gardenia mist gets me in the very face, and I shudder in miasmic delight, dreaming of spring in Shanghai. The heavy traffic around me then dulls to a complete dead stop, and I canter forward toward Yeo's to get my daily dose of palatial dim sum and other fare. As I run forward, I see the centime figures of Chinatown moving like crickets on a turnstile, dancing for joy in the roving belladonna light. There are no reasons, so to speak, why I come here other than to capture that pederast of my youth, so exotic are the looks I get that my skin turns graze green in the bonny afternoon on the spur.

***

Later on that night, with the chrysanthemum perfume sprayed around my ears, piquing my inner senses, I fall asleep dreaming of the seven dynasties, of many fabled ships sinking on disparate rose-colored seas, and of white heron shrieking into the distance. I see the handsome faces of many men kissing my toes and pulling out my long hair, hear the song of the monkey-men teasing me, saying I'm no good, and see a flower-crazy maiden with dimmed sensibilities living on the cusp of only oblivion. Clangor of the snake pot, pupil of the mint caterpillar eye, temple of faraway picaresque . . . There are devilish ghosts haunting me at every turn, screaming out at me in my forgotten freesia dreams, calling me a vamp and a hussy, a destitute princess who is fed up with the times. When I awaken in the night, I'm covered with hot sweat, looking into the mirror only to see my eyes vacant like glassy windows of shame, tousled like a wild banshee to be sure.

After that, I begin to demur and think of the other personals in my life and run to the door of my house for breath, a muse claustrophobic washing over me. Awake in my mind were those heady days of grandeur I felt before I came to C-town, fallen days of cricket and cricket. It was the pulse of demagoguery in me that led me to believe something fictive about my life, to cling to the city for all it was worth, to run down the dragon villa with an undisputed passion of the gods and a full truss of golden words, vocabulary that miffed the ego and turned sweet in the lonesome fog along the famous bridge. It's then I see the nocturnal gypsy again turning round and round with her toothless aphrosy, gaping at my full-bodied stare, aping my foodles with disintegrating ardor in high spirits, and asking me if I'm that okay.

My usual reply is always the same these days. It's this place called Monkey-town I desire, the outlay of the forgotten city, the V-stitch I cling to like a lost Girl Scout badge of honor that makes my sash dissolve with kaleidoscope colors, some crystalline eyes of the woman derides me and says it's foolish to be so stubborn on a city so filled with golden Buddha legs and hotch kiss splendor of your early killjoy days.

I crave it nonetheless and divulge my heart, preferring soggy crab and dumplings, the shadows on Walter L. Lum place, making me feel eerie. If I had no other preference, why not follow the bells and smells there and look for those lost parakeet eyes?

***

On a sobriquet Sunday, I reach for my favorite magazine and give the glossy a read, dreaming of all those sensational words dashing through my head, the stand-out pics of aromatic shrimp paste in round bamboo steamers emanating through each advertisement like some dint of my heritage that makes my mouth water endlessly. If it's not this, it's that. With some respect, I sneer at the brittle bottle of chrysanthemum perfume sitting on my desk, which is shaped like a bawdy lady's body, and admit that I've dreamt sixteen pornographic dreams in black and white ever since I've doused the stuff between my daffy ears.

"Shame on you!" I can see the shaman screaming at me, looking repulsed, and warning me to beware of the weird vernal magic that vendors do. "They try to steal your heart and put it in their tiny, obscene locket. Chrysanthemum perfume? Pooh-pooh! It's no more than mere gorilla stink!"

What guides me in my discovery of the famed city? It's that pervasive shriller, its braided tenements, the doo-wop nightlife so clear to see in the universal glass olive-scented mai tai which dances in my fingers. Fair-weather trophies and flossy Japanese paper umbrellas which don't fold up correctly, which put you under the *spell*. It's the hiss of the dragon ganglia in these lovely gotcha villa stores which will make your finical eyes go agog, as if you're maniacal as a blowfish, snow-driven, about to expel into another courtly dimension. Dimpled porcelains and the chit-eyed dinosaurs which are stuffed with raw copper coins are the heyday of some inventive daydream, some fixative eye pose which bandies about in frozen midair.

As I slide my fingers across the must-have keyboard, it goes *bleep* in the stream of jetty, leaving me breathless and hopeless as a young child again, playing peekaboo with the many neon green papaya signs that twinkle in the bright horizon on a horny hinge.

Kearny, Washington, Canal, these too I mouth off from memory, remembering the suspicious woman who sold me the chrysanthemum perfume, nothing so wonderful as being a romantic in the twenty-first century as walking in the tandem square of Chinese enlightenment. I see a seer wearing a tacky pastel hat warning me of my heresy in the veering sunlight, her speech peppered with the kind fluted words of the heretic. She speaks of wontons, gummy tea, and all that goose talk, says I'll never make it past the front gate entrance of Chinatown without being eaten up by curlews. Her very words singe and make me double over like carrefour, some suggestion of chewed-up bubblegum in the seams of the sidewalk looking starched-heavy and leaving my very eyes impregnated with a curious poison.

"Why try so hard to fit in the crowd when the crowd isn't made for you?" she says with gaping lava teeth, looking humorously at me as she preaches from the inside of the Shiseido store with the mauve umbrella front. "What you have is the strangest skin ever, and you need to be put in clinkers!"

As she chastises me for being such a goony, she explains to me that Chinatown is a land of segue and plenty, that she can *smell* it on me, some seminary impulse that makes me more iconoclastic and ridden with the rotten, some double-helix-driven words that are sure to leave me in the box if I'm not careful. The pearl-scented city is made for party wreckers and glorified lizard eaters, full bingers, and majestic card holders, some limb-of-the-tree fantasy flingers that want to use all five fingers when they eat their dim sum. Not just any old suds chopsticks fantasy but the whole beach rigmarole, mind you, she says, rolling her eyes facetiously, picturing a tea shop where the people come and go exposing their better tattoos and taboos in favor of all that barley talk. An eternal place where the parlor leaves will glow like the bicuspid from other planets, and the tea will spigot from the nostrils of reindeer. In those places, conversation might flow like champagne from a spider's eyelash or a torp of a tender one, some overripe dignitary from another country playing pansy with your eyes and just the disco music you've always longed for tumbling through your tunnel ears.

****

Sometime later, I discover, hours later, as I check my dresser drawer, there's a note, to my surprise, that says, "Go to the Bamboo Villa right away to see the Mr. Fong! Urgent business!"

I quickly put my rubbed-up coat and scarf on and hop into my car and begin to press the gas pedal hard, getting on the freeway, driving past the many pseudo-colored cars that resemble tanks and rabbits moving in a hypnotic blur. The AM radio blasts the morning news, some inveterate buzz, and hum of the hazy world which is at once a hymn of rupee and trivial chatter. What is it that the outrageous Mr. Fong could possibly want at this time of day? And why should he call on me again and again?

As I move onto the freeway onto streamline 101, I begin to dream of Chinatown superior, of the rice hounds who go there, of the still-life friezes of gentility in their long vacation shirts that blow ecstatic finicky bubbles in the air, of all that old Confucian gentility and order moving and changing into a chain of discotheques. It's all a cloud of disparu to me, this particular psychobabble of ever-fading grace, those cynical eyes pondering another day of carefree wandering about Waverly Place, the clubby knickknacks you can buy for a mere fifty cents in your shoulder bag. It's all mix and match, up and up, a mixed-up ghetto of new and old life with elongated red and gold letters, some Sino-hub from the stars, mongering like a land of plenty.

As I pass up another car on the freeway, there begins another daydream of the many animated faces I've met in this hub of aggregate C-town, of Flora and Mr. Fong, of their wonderful duo romance, of Alicia and Ming and the baby they've just had, and of Mrs. Wong and her sub-angular anxiety. Like big bubblegum faces blowing in the wind, a desideratum of deep love and passion, these bloated personas of Chinatown hiss to me their secret lives on the monochrome dashboard and drown out the AM radio, mocking the announcer with his loud, pompous static words of aquatic grief.

As the clouds lift up ahead, I'm reminded of my earlier days of childhood, of those angst-ridden teenage bebop melodies that will crop up on the dial now and then, full of bawdy notes and romantic sensibilities. Some knock-down spoony tunes that will make you break down with hillbilly laughter. I begin to think of love affairs I've had in the past, of sometime amours that have made me happy as a clam and then have given me nightmares. All those surging memories come fading back as I make my way into Chinatown down to Jackson Place where I cruise by and see people marching back and forth in their black garb, hear the shaman preaching, and listen to the monk bang his gong like a big drum of hollow reverberations. A virtual circus for the gut killer, a Chinese up in arms in high-style confetti. The very picture of the holy convent of disbelief.

***

It was that enlightened yellow light that was chasing the city in two per colors, some beat of the street that drove the people wild and made the tourists look wide-eyed at the little plastic Bodhisattvas that were the size of honey jars in the fantastical shops on Geary Street. Some pennies stuck to the bottom of their shoes that made them think twice of walking faster into the intemperate love zone. Some wildish endeavors of the lonely crowd that made them scribble moonshine on the walls of happy graffiti where the smell of *kung pao chicken* was wafting to and fro, the furlough leaves of plane trees were earthbound, and the slight prattling of children were known. The beetle keepers and their gnarly zeroes moved on the planet with a surly one-two, and the catfish tendrils took a weave into the sketchy air. Damper shadows moved with alarming beat into the deathly quiet parts of the city and were rewarded with shogun colors; there were disparate remarks about the condition of the people. Beautiful and pseudo-eccentric with a sudsy hue and sentimental eyes, they walked the feathers of the lone synchronicity in the air—making amok the scatter-brained flashes of the orioles. Those subsun colors of the oriental creatures and their shadows—somewhat like the tortuous shades of amber I once knew as a child.

Of aspidistras and sintered diamond effect, of lightning fast solos of the planets, of footsteps leading to Mars and beyond those stars. Those tripod notes of sorrow of the travel to space when we listen to them too deeply by the newspaper stand, which is just a juicy inkblot tall, the midget man juggling his wares in the squirrelly wind with a spider cap on. What with this celebratory effect his million character bits have on us, like gorilla print for the weathered, busy eyes, while nearby someone makes winter melon soup with a hint of zappy infusion of salts, a sniggering of mean-faced Cantonese men walking about with their poppy sleeves on fire. "What's the state of politics in Hong Kong and Taiwan?" asks one demon-mouthed meddler at the booth. "I don't know, and I don't care," spits the angry two-fisted scholar in the ramen restaurant, slurping his noodles most unctuously. Surely a big to-do. These people are all about the yin and yang of things, some loud apathy and some hot flashes, some apocalyptic genius in the waiting wings about to spring out like counting sarsaparilla.

"I'll have you know that Monkey-town is, in effect, a city of dark vision and lost respect—a culled-out bungalow of foolish dreams! It's the beginning and end of all things!" the old woman says with a sad sigh, stirring her Horlicks with a genteel spoon.

"Can't you see—you've come so far to see the city and its busybodies eating their radish cakes with their plum-sauce noses hooked up in the air. What you find is that nobody gives a shit about your world vision!" says Mr. Choy, the tailor, shaking his head and saying *tsk, tsk* at the mourning passersby.

As I move about, the countless people of Monkey-town seem like screaming pedants in a lost dream, all vying for a sinking glossy jade in a vast pond of waves. What could I know of their happiness and sorrow, of their *sine qua nons,* and of their tomorrows, their musical loves, and their choice syncopated vim? I yawn inwardly and take in the whole fragrant city with its bloodred buildings and its fringed obelisk lanterns like a tattered subway postcard and dream of that Shangri-La beyond, of flying cranes and sparkling lotus ponds. So comforting is the song of the *chit chit* of the miniature parakeet in outer paradise, of the denizens in regal purple threads milling about that I smile then to myself and confess

Monkey-town is indeed that silvery ingot of enlightenment I have been looking for all my life. Why look deeper than the misfit powers of the goose-necked children and the sampan flurries of the well-dressed dozen?

***

At noon time at Yeo's, they sit—Flora and Mr. Fong—in the frozen walls of the painted sampan room, face to face, eating their parsed-out dim sum like two befuddled birds huddled closely, flirting with each other with winsome words about the lost syllable time, conversing with the glowing diamond as a present stuffed in Flora's slim hand. With some exotic patterned duo rose sat the lacy cut hem of her long dressing gown and her hair done up like a shiny bouffant of spiraled joy, Flora shrugs and winces her elongated nose a bit and uses her ivory chopstick to helicopter-dive into the shrimp body of a *har gow,* causing the hot oil to refract a thousand glissomes. "It's this, our little snail of gorgeous contempt!" she jibes him, biting in with both bone white teeth as if to demolish the little white body.

"If you're to have *har gow,* you must have its pair—the trumpet of Asia, the royal snout—the *sui mai!*" Mr. Fong jibes facetiously, putting a snivel of pork dumpling in her plate and yelping loudly like a wily hyena in high contemptible druthers.

Twisting her hair in her hand, the lovely Flora demurs and lets the tiny pork shard fall into her round porcelain bowl and makes a strimping noise that miffs her. Verily, she had been dreaming for some time of running off to Hong Kong, Hawaii, or some other exotic place. Why Monkey-town, with all its hungry minions, was starting to get to her, to nettle her with its run-of-the-mill eyesores? She liked to say she was entranced by Mr. Fong's handsome face, large watery eyes, and charismatic wisdom words, and she couldn't stand another day in the everyday flower business!

"Why not this octopus pudding, darling dear?" she said, digging into the next dish with droll, vapory expression which wandered a bit. "They always serve it with a hint of burnt chicory, just the way you like it!" She secretly doted on him but suddenly found the hideous and unexpected pith on his dreary nose to be a bit off-putting.

"I prefer the sesame ball, but thank you," Mr. Fong replied abruptly and coldly in return, guessing what she thought with some hint of sarcasm. As a monomaniac with an ideogram on his nose that he thought resembled something out of the ordinary out of the movies, he felt himself charmed and could read minds! He didn't like to be so viewed with a microscope of the second stripe.

"You'll never guess what Alicia is up to now—she's been very mysterious of late," said Mr. Fong, suddenly raising his wine cup and changing the subject in a ploy to gain favor and attention. He longed for Flora's well-set eyebrows, her rubylike lips, and her attractive nose. How he hated it when she made fun of his hairy pith and intimated that she wanted to run off to Hong Kong, of all places! Women were such explosive powder kegs of joy and doom! He wanted to hear none of it sometimes! Only to have some sup-sup and to make milder merry was his wont!

"How so? Mysterious? I've heard that that she's become some famous bitch! Ming has stopped gambling too and stays home and dotes on the bratty child, and the woman just runs around town looking sooty and full of bravado! I believe the woman spends her time in a disco parlor now."

"How lousy of her, and the kid only two years old! He's going to turn out to be a real lunatic! Not a grade A fob like yourself, darling."

At the sound of this compliment, he picked up the diamond and flashed it winningly in front of her eyes and gulped, expressing a *gosh, jolly* attitude that mesmerized her and made her forget her abject cynicism and fall in love with him. His pith, previously hideous, suddenly become a spigot of joy and a shimmering thread of due exultation. She longed to tug on it generously with a zap.

As Mr. Fong made joyous fishlike noises with the burble of his lower lip, he did his Elvis impersonation, as he always did when he was with her, and made fun of all the people he knew in Monkey-town, gossiping with such splendor that the patient hours rolled by with ease.

"That's my Weldon!" Flora tittered, biting into the octopus pudding with sometime glee, which he now took part in with severe gluttony, burping like a mean fiend of the true moment. It was that heady chemistry which drew them together, an admixture of tongues and winning eyes that Cantonese love to commingle over extraneous worlds and naughty vices which make the world spin ever so fast.

***

PART V

THE CHANT

With snakelike eyebrow tattoo that is as becoming as her mysterious inner light, Alicia stands in a low-cut lime green dress the color of melting leaves, with the glowing spotlight on her at the Blue Dragon Lair; the bulbs dimmed low to the tilt of her deepest fantasies. Just as she finishes bolting out the last cadenza of "Unchained Melody", the rapt audience in the background rises to their hushed feet and gives her a standing ovation to the fore, with pressed tears in their spurious, welled-up eyes.

"That takes the cake. It's the best you've ever done!" screamed Mr. Lau who had in his hand a dozen florid red roses and a paycheck. "How about a kiss, Alicia?"

Breathless, holding the microphone still, the young Alicia is stunned to her senses, unable to comprehend how it was that she was able to sing so freely in front of so many hair-brained people and not faint away without a whist. The wife of a scholar in front of all these people doing show business! Who was to think of anything so absurd or painfully out of the ordinary at that?

It had suddenly started two months ago, during a hot dry spell in August, when she was just going out to pick up Daniel from the playground and buy some eggs on the spur to the market. On her way to the grocery store, she had chipped her shoe and found a strange, handsome man looking at her lasciviously who turned out to be Roger Lau, the owner of that famed nightclub in Chinatown, the Blue Dragon Lair.

"I've heard so much about you!" she tittered, laughing at the top of her lungs, flattered to be noticed by such a handsome man. Surely this might upset Ming!

"And I you!" the man said, laughing, elbowing her aside quickly so the customers could buy their sundry things in the supermarket aisle without jostling one another.

"You're the daughter of Old Lady Wing, the one who was so charmingly sentimental that they threw roses at you at your wedding! There was a fracas after that!"

"Enough said. And your nightclub a fabulous success!"

"That's all proper flattery on your part!"

"And yours too, my love."

After what was a long silence and a hideous torture, Roger broke out. "Listen, can you sing? I mean *really* sing? We need talent in there like hell, and I like your style. How about you show up at our nightclub and give it a *bang*?"

"What in the hell are you talking about, sir?"

"I mean would you like to perform at our club?"

It was true that Alicia was known in the city to be a talented karaoke singer and could perform many popular singing numbers, but the very idea of being an actual club performer stunned her and made her heart beat quickly out of meager tempo. All those people out there in the audience gawking at her with grimacing eyes. What would Ming then think? Would he succumb to approve?

Now as she stood there in the fuzzy white lights of the jazz club, her wavy hair glistened with cool melodrama and her fairy-tale eyes wandered about the room until they settled on Mr. Fong who was sitting in his green absurd fedora, smoking a long black Cheever's pipe and making *goo-goo* eyes at her. The impervious old Mr. Fong who was the principled anchor of Monkey-town, who said silly, pedantic things and made people cackle like foreign cockatoos, who had brown gunny-sack skin and dreamy, unkempt ideas, who made improper gestures like a hang-me-up puppet and spoke of far-off penumbras. What could the puckish Mr. Fong be possibly thinking of at this time of the night?

"You've done it now, Alicia! That Ming of yours will never forgive you. How could you have sung so well? You're a rising star. A toast to you!" he sang out boisterously and burped three times with his mai tai in his hand, bumping the diner next to him facetiously on the rump.

"Mr. Fong, you are too much. How can I ever repay you for your gratitude and support? Where is Flora?"

"Flora is off getting her hair done, ta-ta! And you don't have to repay me, darling. Just go on being your beautiful strange self, and don't ever change." He patted his button-up cap with due satisfaction and looked at her with gleaming, irreproachable eyes that spun round and round like a toaster frog.

"I won't, Mr. Fong. I promise!" As she hugged her damp bouquet of roses to her chest, she winked at Roger and hurried out the door in the falling glamorous rain, singing a refrain from her last show tune and suddenly felt a horrendous tinge of guilt come upon her like the plague. What would her husband Ming say? *It surely was not as if he cared anyways,* she thought to herself sleepily, dreaming of Roger's eyes naughtily and slipping down Battery Street past the subway station and schoolyard and a line of yew trees, padding her feet on the sidewalk. These days had been filled with consternation and meandering on her part. It was just such dumb luck to be singing at the nightclub, to be chosen for such a part! Little did Roger know how she was tickled pink, how it struck her fancy!

When she arrived home, she saw the sleepy faces of Ming and Daniel pressed against the glass windowpane in the rain, their matching imperial brown noses looking so deprived of natural color and warmth that it made her laugh. *Why that, Master Ming?* she thought to herself, sick of his gambling and pedantic ways. As she opened the door, she let out a loud yawn, meant only to be heard by him.

"What's that—you're late again. I heard the neighborhood train pass by twice and didn't sleep. What's wrong with you, and where have you been?"

"I've been singing at the Blue Dragon Lair."

"*Singing!* For Christ's sake! At that pit! What for? It's not like we don't have enough money. I smell something strange on you. Are you in love with someone?"

"No, and stop being so jealous! I just want to sing and see if I have talent."

"Talent, *hmph.* You do seem to have that, in many directions."

"Look, I'm going to be singing there next week, and the week after that, so there's nothing you can do to stop me!"

"Then forget we knew each other!" Ming screams with vicious teeth and tears in his face, slamming the door, scratching his large eyes out.

As Alicia walks away coldly in the other room, all she can hear are the notes of "Unchained Melody" and see the smoke rings of the club in her jetsam face. Although she loves Ming, she can't figure out what's gotten into her! Something about becoming a star or a valise of love has transfixed her eyes. Suddenly Ming and his fuddy-duddy drawings didn't seem that great anymore, and the great lights of the world of the jazz club had entranced her! To think that after all these years, she was finding that her budding voice could move people to hocus-pocus and even rude enlivenment. She didn't know why, but she was settled on her next singing performance, dreaming of the sensational showtime. The big time.

***

Russet-colored leaves, that jaded look on the old man's face with the toothy grin, the lopsided take on the *lapsho-apso* in the corner of the grocery store, the slow-to-growl eyes of the wormy matrons in the grocery store transfix each customer as they get their gluten, their cut fish, and their sacks of short-grain rice, grinning widely like Piccadilly clowns, their ties smashed on nonsensically with a vehement, earthy twist. As the cash register totals up the daily sum, the blue jays cavort with one another on the sidewalk, and Maybelle eats her haw flakes one by one with a red thumb, dreaming they are pennies for the video slot machine at home.

"Your momma is a no-good slut!" she screams to Daniel who sobs by the rocking horse chair looking so angry that even at that age he learns to make dragon fists full of irate fury.

Tomorrow is another day! he thinks, spinning his ball of a fist up in the air like a cannonball. "Don't get in fights with girls. Treat them with respect!" Ming says, patting him on the cap and paying at the grocery line, glaring at Maybelle with a silly laugh. How he misses his art deco drawings which he has left behind in the garage of the house because he's been too depressed to pick up the pen! How he misses the famous gambling houses which treated him with so much admiration.

"Where have you been, Master Ming?" Mr. Yu asks sarcastically outside the grocer stand, a thick wad of dirty wafting bills up his sleeve by his Rolex. His large eyes glitter sensationally like a snake, and he looks haughty as usual, a man-about-town about to go for his daily massage and mah-jongg. "Why aren't you gambling with us, Ming?"

"I've been home taking care of the kid and washing dishes!" he retorts, laughing through his nostrils. "It's a long story."

"We've heard all about it. I go the jazz club on Battery every Wednesday and see your wife perform. She's a knockout. What can we say if we can't keep the missus in bed with you?"

"What the hell do you mean?"

"She's a glamorous piece of action up there. I'd be jealous if I were you!"

"Oh shut up, will you!"

"Anyways, I'll be moseying along now, bucko, but have fun. Just warning you that your wife is turning into some floozie!"

"Mind your own business, and I'll take care of mine!"

As they part ways, Mr. Song, the grocery store owner, winks at Mr. Yu, and they guffaw loudly and exchange joking crude pleasantries in Cantonese, making Ming shake visibly. What was there to say about Alicia performing in a nightclub where all the men could see her? Why was he so disturbed? Could it be that she was really having an affair with Roger Lau, the famed owner?

As he walked down Ocean Street, his eyes met Mrs. Yu in shame, and he kept kicking his sneakers in the heat. He couldn't believe that Alicia would be that way, in a low-cut dress for all the men to gawk at, in a smoky barroom belting out garish songs for people to hear. As if he didn't matter to her at all. The more he thought about it, the more crazy he became, and the more irate he felt.

When he reached home with Daniel, he ran to the garage crying and reached for his pens and began to draw his diagrams again and soon had a whole chest of papers delineating the surface of the moon, of Monkey-town, of the rambling world at large. He couldn't stop scribbling. He took two pills and some Coke and went to bed, dreaming pensively. Surely, anything was better than Alicia performing in a nightclub and flirting with Roger Lau. When he woke up, he tore his drawings apart and cursed himself for being so romantic.

***

Mrs. Wong in a green parakeet hat looking at the flash camera, *voila!* Some scarlet hose and memories worth remembering. The sudsy curls of sampan women are to be relished by dolorous afternoon eyes resting on ungrateful tea cups with silver handles and Western glitter; in the praxis, the downtown jazz music resounds with frenzy, spilling over into other smoky oolong tea rooms, making her squeak with despair, our heroine at last in a wash of color pecking at her sweet meats, a U-line of brimming lustful vanities. What's confusing is the puzzle of her earth wig smile and her beautiful upswings, her beehive tantrums, her highfalutin' politics, and her raucous laughter! How she shimmies to the camera like a slow horse. Voila!

I see her then move and cascade through glossy doorways and lampposts like a revenant without a cause, biting her hard-won glossy nails with gusto, dancing through slim strumpets of fog with airy art and magic. That jazzy remnant in her heart could cause her to falter so, to trace the sublime stars in the darksome eyes of Mr. Wong who was always making mischief. She clung to her dim sum wrappers and made hay, didn't care what other people thought, was always on the cusp of *something.*

Perhaps it was that damned Mr. Fong that deserved to be boiled to death in scarlet cup of tea, she thought cynically, blessing time for its connivance. As she boiled her cache of ginger head tea, she let the puckered tea leaves sough out, a gift from Mrs. Tang whom she anointed with beatific and put her fingers together on the cement table, laughing at some inner cosmic joke of sorts. The truth was, she couldn't stand it any longer, the perennial hi jinx of Monkey-town, the hack games of the lewd pranksters. A place where you couldn't go around smiling at others, to think of it!

She raised her quizzical low-set eyebrows in midair, fidgeted a bit with her Indian pillow, let her head sough to the sound of the Beijing zither in cool play. Surely, the city was becoming a random brouhaha of sorts, a second stripe of the sullen heart. She lay her heavy head on the pillow and allowed the flowing dreams to come, let her hair fall into a chunky mass over the hydra pattern, and let her manifest thoughts trickle over the sundry waterfall . . . Surely many wowsy things were happening all over the city, but she'd always be here in her nook, darning and crocheting and lapping up the electric air with a bit of comeuppance, looking so darling in the secret antechamber, cynically inhaling the black foul oxygen that was meant for her, studying the holy great onyx on her pinky toe, taking a stab at it, *futura,* whatever that meant, if anything. The holy ones were always being preyed upon in Monkey-town like some little fish in a tank, swishing about with glum faces . . . Surely she was no different!

****

Swollen bees, the whirling, intemperate weather charms her. Alicia has no doubts about it that she will be a hit at the microphone again, belting those high notes, *soprano,* in a falsetto of voices that will impress the wild ones of the audience as she has in the previous stunning weeks. With flippant gestures and not a little improvisation, she rolls up her sleeve and imagines the drumroll, sees Fatso by the bar ordering his oeuvre of cocktails with the little colored paper miniature umbrellas in them, sees the breathless faces looking altogether tough and weathered and worn at her as if from a dummy camera, transfixed. It's this vain thing to look together, hypnotic, with two-bit earrings gliding past her ears, to sing *effortlessly.* If only Ming could see her!

Now as the taupe curtains part away, she sashays to the middle of the room to see Fatso ogle her breasts, and she lets out a squeak of hearty disapproval during the first number despite her dramatic moment. She lets out the first trilling notes to "Moon River" and falters, falters again, and then catches herself, sees her reflection in the glass vase on the step of the climbing jazz stairs, and sees Fatso yawn again. *Who is she fooling anyways?* she thinks to herself. She is nothing but a movie star, a leftist fool doing seed work in the heart of Monkey-town, giving those C-town fobbies a run for their money. *Cheap tunes for midnight moments, the twilight touch,* she thinks sarcastically to herself, dreaming of the darned curtain closing, which it does at last.

The cast of the snake drum holds the audience in its thrall, and the dimpled-cheek waiter calls out her very name, swaggering down the mai tai line past the vain ostrich-feathered women who dance, making her giddy in the face. It's been six weeks since her name, Alicia Wing, has been held up in bright-studded lights on the marquee sign. Thanks to Roger; she's become a star.

"I have no idea what I'm doing!" she whines to herself inwardly as she waltzes on stage, brushing a wisp of glowing hair off her fine cheek, flirting with the audience, belting out those high uppity notes with a rapid sigh. When it gets to tough parts, she just fakes out and lets out a rough, raspy laugh, the way she's seen it in the movies. Surely no one could tell!

The butterfly mesdames were gliding behind their solid-gold base fans, batting their glittering eyelashes at her, drinking their pearly drinks with a blasé effect that made her quake, eyeing her coolly. Who was she to sing all these laughable songs with such a lusty voice to pretend she was the next Diana Ross? The old women in the audience shook their heads and made no-no gasping sounds, made their fat pale ankles shake back and forth in the grotesque light while the wild band kept playing at *rat-a-tat-tat*, keeping the dancers in check. The rainbow juicy colors of the discotheque ball kept changing shape with a gaudy coloration and left the bar crowd breathless, ephemeral, and free at last to exchange gossip and hushed veneration.

The squidlike trombone player let out a gust of rushing laughter and scratched his belly and said, "Ain't she pretty?" And he screamed, "Play it again, Gus!" while the whole club sang along, chanting her breathy name.

Alicia sang at the top of her lungs amid whaling and rosy cheers, looking beautiful and robust as ever, her long hair hanging down to her waist covered with a mop of sweat. When she was finished, her famished eyes glistened, and she sat down only to see Ming at the door clapping with tears in his eyes. This was the first time he had been at the Blue Dragon Lair to hear Alicia sing, and he was absolutely astounded. Why that, he thought, was why he loved her and forgave her everything.

***

The silvery shadows of time, encounters in the haze, counterpoint of catfish and seaside melody, the lugubrious thought chasers of the city are met with the aftermath in the heart of the urban sprawl covered with electric lights, the old hats and fedoras of that color wasted by another hour flying off to another dimension. I move from my car to the parking lot at Washington Park, admiring the cave man graffiti with an oval eye, distancing myself from the others. The ribboned light cuts like a devilish feeder into the parking lot and leads me into the park where the old dancing bird-faced men are playing chess, configuring the pieces together one by one in world of mayhem and deliberation.

The swinging trees sway back and forth in the purring wind, and I smell the wicker candy in the pockets of the young children who move in their home-knit sweaters the color of earthy rainbows, their eyes like newborn caterpillars on the move. The benches are the color of cherry spritz, and the sun flies down upon the earth like a fresh pillar, full of fragrant salt. Too much to say it, when the Monkey-town mystery will evolve eventually, when the colored socks of the children will change hues in the light, twisting at every angle. The mirrored cloaks of old women with bandages on their feet and washed-out smiles and coals for eyes hug their ferns in their bosoms and lift their shiny pinwheels in the fresh air, screaming *"ai-yeeh!"* With Cantonese that sounds like a trailer machine, the old matrons file their wax nails and drink their milk teas, sounding so corny and fed up with the world, their high-to-shine eyes blinking away hot fog, and their toes dancing in the painted grass. The ostrichlike people dance away beside the red benches and comment on the hazy weather and pinch their noses at the stench of the old fish bones by the garbage can. Punch-heavy, the boulderlike men read their Confucian primers and dream of a decent world run by scholars and chieftains. The ribbons in their eyes look like fresh cream.

I want to walk two more times around the park, take in the whole atmosphere with my flirtatious manner before it disappears into thin air, take out my drawing pad and dabble with colored pens, and capture some spirit before the sun comes down. Why say so much, I think, when it's all there on the faces of the people of the city, brown and cryptic, like proper soy, and frazzled like the spigot of the moon? The order of the denizens came from centuries of love and passion at the rice mill, hours wandering at the *gufu* filling up with chopstick vanity. Why that, I think, is the genius of the warbling hours.

****

The purplish contours of those dreamy hollows left an octopus mark between her teeth, the light cloven between her toes, her weathered eyes a thing of the frivolous imagination. The candied stripe onion in her frying pan left her eyes watering, made the jetsam dots on her blouse darken with color, and made her hospitable face lean sideways in the kitchen. What holy spumes of charcoal smoke sputter between her greased-up fingers into the air, and how she fries her squid cake most deliriously like a sous-chef, basting it with haughty pleasure? How she sings out the hour with music on her pink tongue?

Mrs. Wong deemed it a thing of the past—those irrefutable pleasures of the jazz room, the opium lounge to be taboo, and it haunted her—those inescapable notes in midair. She opened the window to let out the air and gasped readily, admitting that Monkey-town was the magic kingdom in which things could be experienced wholly as a moniker of time. She didn't know how she could make it up to people—apologize to all the personages she had upset in a millennium, sampan bitty with the upright spatula screaming epithets from the stalwart heart. She had lost her bet somehow, burned the squid cake, and left gaping holes of silver in the meat, exposed herself as a fiend of tortuous duty. Oh, beating heart of quiet thunder!

Now, fiend, she wrangled for some dubious identity in the name of sampan love and saw it run free, her good name. What was that extremity that she had pulled off? Some gag or *in extremis* vowel in her throat choking her to death? She wanted to pull the jade ring off her finger and dump it in the frying pan amid all the smoke to choke herself with a sylvan color of sorts. How it pained her, her C-town blues.

"I'll have you know that, that there is no remedy for melancholia!" the shaman had warned her one day by the window, preaching to her with his ready voice, shaming her for her antics. "You have to take the dragon root, but it never works completely. You're just a thimble of disbelief."

Mrs. Wong trembled in her apron and studied the squid cake cautiously, cutting the legs off just so in the silvery light, in quarters, and trounced it with a knife and let loose whoop. If others could be saintly, so could she, go on plodding in this mysterious villa behind closed doors. She

didn't mind and didn't believe she could be anything otherwise. It was all cryptic blather, the outré world: the sprawling vat of disbelief. She would continue to garner mist and opiate roses in this wonderland, culling out those fantasies for herself, if only to mock others. She was, after all, the dragon lady of contempt, the silent glory of the Chinatown muses.

***

Dragon dips in the valley; a voyeur dipped in elusive paints I walk about the city looking frantic, pass the cinnabar streaks on the sidewalk, dreaming of the constant sousing in the bars, the high life of the cinched-eyed centurions. I tug on the Jesus rope, stare at the eclectic tangerine sparks in the sky, see the old man picking at his teeth with greasy fingers like an allegory from an old book. The scene moves me like a panel from fresco. How the doughty rain begins to fall lightly, like flighty goose feathers.

Dabs of alligator paint on my toes, I walk past the grotesque eyeballs around me and dance by the yew trees, pass by the Hotel L'Orange, which I stare at cynically with a twitch of the eye, laughing. Out comes the mighty shaman, in a huff, looking dapper and coolheaded, as if he's smoked a thousand pipes.

"What's that? So you've found your beat and have stopped struggling with the world?" the shaman asks cheekily, walking by me with a hint of outright mystery.

I laugh and say that the past year in Monkey-town flew by so quickly that I was caught unaware in my dreams and was so much departed from my senses that I didn't have time to be so aware of any enlightenment. So much for an inner struggle!

As we walk down Geary, he asks me what I think of all this wonder bluster, these crazy miracles I've witnessed in the fine city, what serious-minded business I've tripped upon, and what thrice-colored characters have come into my queue. It's that characteristic lisp he speaks with that clipped, Cantonese accent that sinks into reverberant waves that beguiles me and breaks into mooselike colors. He looks suddenly evangelically curious. Why Monkey-town, he asks, mocking me like a cool, clean mosquito?

I demur and say I'm just a passerby again and like the sounds and the sights, the run-of-the-mill colors, the way the people garble their athwart fantasies like the gems of the Pacific and tousle their hair under the light with such keen adoration. Something of it brings to me the keen familiarity of home and some kindred delight called the hours of hours. I bring it to the fore and laugh and say it's a piece of my heart, some fractured stumble in the light.

"Oh, that's what you call it. Then you should say you chisel fantasies out of wood! How about this teakwood boat for five cents on Jackson Street? You say that's what you'd like to buy for your grandma?"

"How about that lotus leaf dangler, that juxtaposition piece that steals my heart?" I say smartly.

"You know, Monkey-town is not for the cowardly or for the callow. It's for the saintly. The real wonders of the world happen here!"

"That's true, Master Shaman, which is why I'm laughing with you!"

As we wind up the hill, which resembles a praying mantis, his billowing sleeves hang down from his arms, and he rushes up the slope and points down at the city, just as night is beginning to fall and compasses it, and says, "This is the city of disbelief!"

Down below, the entire Monkey-town lights up like a flashing pinball machine, a Christmas tree in full array, and gapes into the silent night with its astounding relished beauty. There are divine slats of light, a bird call of people like my kind milling about, enjoying the scenery, cursing the drones. All is special brew of fresh starts and new beginnings. Then there is a hush and then just a silent whispery dun.

THE END

CPSIA information can be obtained
at www.ICGtesting.com
Printed in the USA
FSOW02n1616171115
13520FS

9 781503 586826